"I'm Ryan's father. I should have been there."

Hating the look of guilt haunting her eyes, Derrick reached out and pressed his hand over hers. "Bri, this is not your fault." He scraped a hand over his jaw. "And if I'd known about the baby, I would have been there."

"Derrick—"

"No, Bri. It's true and you know it. If I had known, I could have stopped these maniacs from kidnapping my son."

Confusion muddled his brain, panic over where his son was making his throat tight. But Derrick wouldn't let fear consume him.

He'd find Ryan no matter what. And he'd be the father the boy deserved.

RITA HERRON

HIS SECRET CHRISTMAS BABY

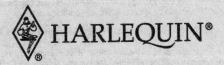

HARLEQUIN®

TORONTO • NEW YORK • LONDON
AMSTERDAM • PARIS • SYDNEY • HAMBURG
STOCKHOLM • ATHENS • TOKYO • MILAN • MADRID
PRAGUE • WARSAW • BUDAPEST • AUCKLAND

To Linda Howard, a special friend of my sister's and now one of mine. Thanks for all your fabulous stories at the mountain cabin in Blue Ridge, and for being a fan! Hope you enjoy this one!

PLEASE RECYCLE · THIS PRODUCT IS RECYCLABLE

Recycling programs
for this product may
not exist in your area.

ISBN-13: 978-0-373-69441-9

HIS SECRET CHRISTMAS BABY

Copyright © 2009 by Rita B. Herron

www.eHarlequin.com

Printed in U.S.A.

ABOUT THE AUTHOR

Award-winning author Rita Herron wrote her first book when she was twelve, but didn't think real people grew up to be writers. Now she writes so she doesn't have to get a *real* job. A former kindergarten teacher and workshop leader, she traded her storytelling to kids for romance, and now she writes romantic comedies and romantic suspense. She lives in Georgia with her own romance hero and three kids. She loves to hear from readers so please write her at P.O. Box 921225, Norcross, GA 30092-1225, or visit her Web site at www.ritaherron.com.

Books by Rita Herron

HARLEQUIN INTRIGUE
  790—MIDNIGHT DISCLOSURES*
  810—THE MAN FROM FALCON RIDGE
  861—MYSTERIOUS CIRCUMSTANCES*
  892—VOWS OF VENGEANCE*
  918—RETURN TO FALCON RIDGE
  939—LOOK-ALIKE*
  957—FORCE OF THE FALCON
  977—JUSTICE FOR A RANGER
1006—ANYTHING FOR HIS SON
1029—UP IN FLAMES*
1043—UNDER HIS SKIN*
1063—IN THE FLESH*
1081—BENEATH THE BADGE
1097—SILENT NIGHT SANCTUARY**
1115—PLATINUM COWBOY
1132—COLLECTING EVIDENCE
1159—PEEK-A-BOO PROTECTOR
1174—HIS SECRET CHRISTMAS BABY**

*Nighthawk Island
**Guardian Angel Investigations

CAST OF CHARACTERS

Brianna Honeycutt—A social worker at Magnolia Manor; her adopted son Ryan is missing....

Derrick McKinney—He'll do anything he can to find the missing child, especially now he knows the baby is his.

Ryan Cummings—The infant has become Brianna's whole world. Why would anyone want to kidnap an innocent baby?

Natalie Cummings—Ryan's birth mother died after childbirth—was it natural causes or was she murdered?

Dana and Robert Philips—They desperately wanted a baby—could they have kidnapped Ryan?

Rhoda Hampton—She recently suffered her third miscarriage—did she take Ryan to replace the baby she lost?

Principal Lamont Billings—Does he know more than he's telling about Natalie's death?

Evan Rutherford—Teacher and high school football coach—does he know who is behind the meth lab?

Jameson Mansfield—The town lawyer who handles adoptions: Does he know something about the missing baby?

Dr. Houston Thorpe—Did he lie about Natalie's cause of death?

Sheriff Beau Cramer—He dated Natalie. But is he covering up her murder?

Mark Larimer—A nurse at the local hospital—did he kill Natalie and kidnap the baby to keep his long-time secret about the meth lab?

Ace Atkins—Is this tough kid from Magnolia Manor responsible for the meth lab?

Prologue

"Brianna, I'm afraid. If anything happens to me," Natalie Cummings whispered, "promise me that you'll take care of the baby."

"Nothing is going to happen to you." Brianna Honeycutt squeezed her best friend's hand as she pulled into the hospital emergency room entrance.

Another contraction seized Natalie, and she began the Lamaze breathing exercises, her hold on Brianna's hand tightening painfully. "He, he, he—ho."

Brianna breathed with her, grateful they'd finally made it to the hospital. A winter storm had rolled in, snow flurries blurring visibility, and she'd had to drive at a snail's pace. And Natalie's contractions were coming one on top of the other.

She threw the car into park as the contraction eased, and helped Natalie out, but Natalie clutched her hand again. "Promise me, Bri, I need to hear you say it."

Pain and fear darkened Natalie's eyes, and Brianna's stomach clenched. She'd known Natalie was afraid of childbirth, but her voice quivered with terror.

"Of course, I will," Brianna vowed softly. "But you're going to be fine. A few minutes from now, you'll be holding your baby, and you'll forget all about the pain."

Natalie opened her mouth to say something, but another contraction seized her. She pressed her hand to her stomach, and tried to breathe through it.

Suddenly a nurse and orderly appeared and raced toward them. "She's in labor," Brianna stated.

The nurse called for a wheelchair, and the orderly ran to get it. Brianna followed behind her as they wheeled Natalie to the reception desk to check her in.

Then suddenly Natalie cried out in pain, her water broke and chaos descended.

"I'm her labor coach," Brianna informed as they rushed Natalie through the double doors to the exam room.

"We'll come and get you in a moment," the nurse said over her shoulder. "Let the doctor examine her."

Brianna nodded, her nerves on edge as her friend disappeared through the doors, a terrified expression on her pale face. Brianna paced the waiting room for twenty minutes, her anxiety rising with every second that ticked by. Finally, her patience snapped, and she rushed to the nurses' station and asked for an update.

The nurse appeared irritated at first, but went to the back to check, then returned five minutes later with a frown on her face. "I'm sorry, miss, but your friend had complications. They've taken her to surgery for an emergency C-section."

A sense of fear overwhelmed Brianna. "Please let me know when she's out."

The nurse nodded, and Brianna paced the waiting

room again. Two other couples hurried in and were sent to birthing rooms, the minutes dragging by. The coffee grew cold, her body more tense as she waited.

What was taking so long? What were the complications? Was Natalie all right? What about the baby?

An hour later, a doctor appeared, the grave expression on his face sending a chill down Brianna's spine. "I'm Dr. Thorpe. You came in with Miss Cummings?"

Brianna nodded, then swallowed and finally forced her voice to work. "The baby—"

"Is fine," the doctor said. "A little boy. Seven pounds, eight ounces. He's in the nursery."

She sucked in a harsh breath and gripped his arm. "And Natalie? Please, I have to see her."

"I'm sorry," he answered quietly. "But your friend died in childbirth."

The room swirled around Brianna in a sea of white, and she felt her legs buckling. The doctor coaxed her to a vinyl sofa, and she put her head down between her knees, afraid she would pass out.

"What happened?" Brianna asked.

The doctor shifted and looked away. "She started hemorrhaging, then her heart gave out."

Her heart? Natalie hadn't had a heart condition, had she?

"Miss Honeycutt, I'm sorry. Is there any family I can call?"

Tears blurred her eyes as she lifted her head to look at him. "No," she whispered. "Just me. I'm her family."

"How about the baby's father?"

"He's not in the picture," Brianna replied.

"Do you know his name so we can contact him?"

"No, she never told me."

"Then we'll need to call social services about the baby."

Panic shot through Brianna, grief, fear and shock in its wake. No, she wouldn't turn the baby over to the system. But Natalie hadn't signed any papers giving her legal custody.

What if the baby's father found out about him? Would he want the baby?

She had to act fast. She was a social worker for the local adoption agency, and she worked with Magnolia Manor, the local orphanage. Natalie wanted her to raise the baby, and she would push through the adoption immediately and keep her promise even if she had to fudge papers to do so.

But Natalie's pleas before she'd gone to delivery taunted her. It was almost as if she'd known that she might not make it.

Had Natalie been afraid of something—or somebody? Had she been in danger?

Chapter One

Six weeks later

"Why can't Robert and I adopt Natalie Cummings's baby?" Dana Phillips asked.

Brianna tensed at the cold hardness in the young woman's eyes. Dana and her husband had been trying to get pregnant for three years, had tried fertility treatments and in vitro fertilization but none of it had worked. Worse, they had been on the adoption list for two of those stressful years.

"You said you'd find us a baby," Dana screeched, "but you've done nothing to help us. And now there's a baby we could have and you won't give him to us."

Brianna understood their desperation, but Dana's emotional state worried her. The woman was obsessed with having a child to the point that Brianna worried about placing one with her.

"I'm sorry, Dana, but Ryan is not up for adoption."

Dana crossed her arms, tears glittering in her eyes. "Why not? His mother is dead, and he has no father. And don't forget, I grew up in this town. I know that Natalie's family is gone now."

Grief for Natalie was still so raw that Brianna's throat thickened with emotions. The fact that Natalie had been anxious her last few weeks and seemed frightened gnawed at Brianna. Women dying during childbirth were uncommon these days. Had Natalie really had heart failure?

"You know I'm right," Dana said, her shrill voice yanking Brianna from the worry that something hadn't seemed truthful about the doctor's explanation.

"I understand that you've waited a long time, Dana, but Natalie asked me to be guardian of her child, and I promised her I would."

"You would be taking good care of him if you gave him to us," Dana pleaded.

"But Natalie wanted *me* to raise him." Brianna reached for Dana to calm her, but Dana jumped up and paced across Brianna's office, her anger palpable.

"Listen, Dana, I know you're desperate, but we'll find you a child. I promised Natalie that I would raise Ryan, though. Natalie was like a sister to me. I have to keep that promise." Besides, the moment she'd held the newborn, she'd fallen in love with him.

"That little boy deserves to have a mother and a father, Brianna, and you can't give him that. You're not even married."

Brianna sucked in a sharp breath. "Dana, I'm not going to argue with you. I've already legally adopted Ryan. Believe me, it's what Natalie wanted."

"It's what *you* wanted," Dana said in a high-pitched

Then one day he'd realized that drinking himself to death was too easy. He needed a clear head to remember what he'd done wrong, and he'd spend the rest of his life trying to make up for it.

Over the next hour, they reviewed office business, salary, benefits and other candidates Gage had brought into the agency. Slade Blackburn, agent. Benjamin Camp, a computer and tech specialist. Levi Stallings, former FBI profiler. Brock Running Deer, an expert tracker. Caleb Walker had special skills that he didn't elaborate on. Colt Manson, a guns and weapons specialist. And he was trying to recruit a woman named Amanda Peterson, a renowned forensic anthropologist. Caleb and Colt hadn't started yet, but Levi, Ben and Brock were on board.

"Do we have a case now?" Derrick asked.

Gage fingered a file. "Not at the moment. I sent Slade Blackburn to recover a young teenager who ran away. He called and will be bringing her back soon."

"Sounds good."

Gage nodded. "Yeah. The mother is a local, Carmel Foster. She'll be thrilled to have her daughter, Julie, back home with her."

"That's what it's all about," Derrick said. "Connecting families."

A smile curved Gage's mouth. "Exactly. But we're still growing the agency. I'd like you on board."

Derrick shrugged. "Hell, a few days off won't hurt me. But I am ready to go back to work, just in case you're wondering."

"I have no doubt." Gage stood. "In fact, that's why I

wanted you here now. Leah and I plan to take a little second honeymoon. Ruby is staying with a friend. I need you to hold down the fort."

"I appreciate the opportunity," Derrick said. "I won't let you down."

Derrick shook his hand again, then strode down the steps and walked out into the cool December air. Christmas was coming, the town was lit up with decorations, winter on its way.

But the holidays had never been high on his list. He'd seen too much over the years, had lost faith too damn long ago to think about singing Christmas carols or shopping.

Besides, he had no one to shop for. No one to celebrate with. No one to share a cozy dinner or decorate a stupid tree.

And that was fine with him.

He climbed in his Jeep, stopped by the florist, picked up a bouquet of lilies, and drove to the cemetery on the edge of town. The little white church needed paint, but vibrant colors from the stained glass windows danced in the waning sunlight across the parched grass and dead leaves. Snow fluttered from the sky in a light downfall, sticking to branches and painting the graveyard in a soft white that made the grounds look almost ethereal, a contrast to the sadness there. A small blue sedan was parked in front of the church, and he wondered if it belonged to the minister or another visitor, but dismissed it without thought.

Tugging his coat around him, he walked through the cemetery searching for Natalie's marker. Sprays of flowers circled a grave in the distance, and he instantly realized it had to be hers. A lone figure stood beside it, burrowed in a coat, head bowed.

He hesitated for a moment, then curiosity overcame him, and he picked his way through the rows of graves until he was close enough to see the figure more closely.

The woman wore a long black coat, and as she leaned forward to place the flowers in the vase at the head of the marker, he spotted a bundle in her arms.

A baby wrapped in a blanket.

The two of them looked like angels in the midst of the snow, like a mirage so beautiful it couldn't be real.

Then she turned to leave, and he sucked in another pain-filled breath.

It was Brianna Honeycutt, Natalie's best friend. Brianna, beautiful Brianna. Brianna with the raven hair and sky blue eyes. Brianna with a voice that sounded like sugar and spice and everything nice. Brianna with skin like a porcelain doll, and a body like a goddess.

Brianna who'd never wanted anything to do with him.

Her face registered shock as she spotted him, and instant regret slammed into him. He'd never had the courage to talk to her when he was young.

Then he'd slept with her best friend, a night that was a blur. Natalie had been in Raleigh, and they'd run into each other at a bar. He'd been upset about a case, and she'd had a sympathetic ear.

Too many drinks later, and they'd ended up in bed. But they'd both known it meant nothing and had gone their separate ways.

Judging from the glare Brianna sent him, she knew exactly what had happened that night and didn't think too highly of him.

His gaze dropped to the baby, and shock hit him. Brianna had a child? He hadn't heard that she'd gotten married.

A quick check to her finger and he saw there was no ring.

"You have a child?" he asked, wondering who Brianna was involved with.

She hesitated, her look wary, then stroked the baby's dark blond head. "I adopted Natalie's son. It was what she wanted."

A knot settled in his gut. He had kept up with the town through the online news and knew that she'd died in childbirth. "Of course."

Then the date of Natalie's death flashed into his head, and the months fell away as he ticked them off in his head.

The dark blond hair... Hair just like his.

Was it possible that that baby was his?

BRIANNA CLUTCHED BABY RYAN to her, a frisson of alarm ripping through her at the sight of Derrick McKinney.

That same feeling of hopeless infatuation she'd felt as a young girl followed. Hopeless because he'd never even noticed her.

Just as she remembered, he was tall, muscled and broad-shouldered. The wind tossed his wavy dark blond hair across his forehead, snow dotting his bronzed skin. His eyes were the color of espresso, a magnetic draw to them that made her body tingle with want. She could still see him dressed in all black, tearing around the mountain roads on that Harley.

Sexuality leaked from his pores just as masculinity radiated off his big body. But even as need and desire swirled through her, fear sank like a rock in her stomach.

He suddenly stalked toward her, his jaw clenched, his eyes darkening as they raked over her and settled on the bundle in her arms.

She'd wondered who the baby's father was, and had feared it might be Derrick, but Natalie had insisted he wasn't. Besides, he hadn't been in Natalie's life the last nine months, nor had he attended the funeral, so she'd assumed that if he was the father, he didn't want anything to do with the little boy.

"Brianna."

She stiffened. His voice sounded rough and deep, the sensuality in his tone igniting desire inside her.

She had to get a grip. Had to steel herself against him. He'd slept with her best friend—*not her.*

And she couldn't forget it.

Tears pricked her eyelids as she zeroed in on the bouquet in his hands. He'd even brought Natalie fresh flowers.

Lilies—Brianna's favorite.

Natalie had loved roses.

God, she was pathetic. Jealous over her friend because Derrick had obviously loved her.

He cleared his throat. "I was sorry to hear about Natalie. How tragic."

Brianna couldn't speak. Instead she swallowed back

tears. As if the baby overheard the reminder that his mother was gone, he whimpered and began to fuss.

"I know how close you two were." He shifted awkwardly on the balls of his feet. "This must be really hard for you."

She nodded. "I still can't believe she's gone. I miss her every day."

His gaze dropped to the fussing baby in her arms. "So Natalie had a little boy?"

Brianna took a deep breath and tugged the blanket over his face to ward off the wind. Or was it so he couldn't see the little boy's face? "Yes."

"What about the father?" Derrick's voice warbled slightly over the word *father.*

Wariness filled Brianna, and she rocked the baby, trying to soothe him. "He's not in the picture."

Derrick's broad jaw tightened. "Where is he?"

"I don't know," Brianna said, trying to stick as close to the truth as possible. "Natalie never told me."

Surprise registered on Derrick's face. "I thought you two shared everything."

At one time they had. But Natalie had glossed over the details of that night with Derrick. And the last few weeks she'd acted strangely, secretive, even shut her out.

Because Derrick was the father of her son? Because she knew it would hurt Brianna even more to know that Natalie shared a child with the only guy she had ever wanted?

"WHAT IS THE BABY'S NAME?" Derrick asked.

Brianna licked her lips, snowflakes dotting her silky

shoulder length hair. "Ryan. It was Natalie's father's name."

He nodded. The Cummings family had been a surrogate to Brianna.

A stiff wind picked up, swirling snow, leaves and dried pine straw around them. Brianna shivered, the baby's cries escalating.

"I'd better get him out of the weather," she said. Then she gave a pointed look at the flowers. "And I'll leave you alone to speak to Natalie."

Cuddling the crying infant to her, she dashed past him, picking up her pace and practically running toward her vehicle. He frowned, a knot gathering in his stomach.

Brianna had always avoided him, but for a moment, he thought he'd detected fear in her eyes.

No, not Brianna. She was as sweet as they came.

Too sweet for his badass ways back then, and too sweet now.

Don't trust a woman, his inner voice warned. Didn't you learn your lesson before?

He walked over and knelt at Natalie's grave, then laid the spray of flowers on the top. "Natalie, is that little boy mine? And if he is, why the hell didn't you tell me?"

He turned and watched as Brianna sped away, and anger began to simmer inside him. He'd never considered having a family, especially a child. Had never thought he'd be any good at it.

But if that baby boy was his, he'd find out.

BRIANNA WAS SHAKING AS SHE drove back to her house, but with the snow thickening, she forced herself to drive slowly and to avoid the dangerous patches of black ice.

What if Derrick was Ryan's father?

Would he want the baby?

An ache rolled through her chest at the thought of having to give up the little boy she'd come to think of as her son. Yet at the same time, guilt pressed against her chest.

She loved Ryan and as his adoptive mother, she had to think about his future, to put him first. She'd never known her own father.

Didn't Ryan have a right to know his, especially if the man wanted to be in the picture?

She parked, gathered Ryan from the backseat, rocking him as she rushed to her house and unlocked the door.

The wind sent the chimes into a soft musical symphony, her front porch swing swaying in the breeze. The wreath she'd hung on the door reminded her of the upcoming holiday, that this was a special time of year. Natalie had loved Christmas.

For Brianna, it had meant lonely nights, holidays without gifts, a reminder that her mother had dumped her on the doorstep of an orphanage and never looked back.

But Natalie had treated her like family, and her parents had included her in their family celebrations, making memories that had changed her life. She and Natalie had decorated cookies together as kids, had created hand-made ornaments and strung popcorn for the tree.

Natalie would be missed.

Brianna would carry on those traditions with Natalie's son, and make sure he knew his mother's love.

Ryan's cries escalated. She flipped on a light and rushed to get him a bottle. He calmed as he ate, and stared at the twinkling Christmas tree lights as if mesmerized by the bright colors. She had bought a crib for the spare bedroom, so she changed his diaper and settled him into the baby bed.

Exhausted herself, she went to her room across the hall, then pulled on warm flannel pj's and climbed in bed.

But worry kept her tossing and turning for hours, her nights filled with memories of the orphanage and the friend who'd left her behind.

Then other images taunted her. Derrick's big masculine body. Derrick looking at her with desire. Touching her. Wanting her. Making her his.

Finally she fell into a deep sleep, but a noise jarred her awake.

The baby crying…. He was probably hungry again.

She shoved the covers aside, jammed her feet into her slippers and pulled on her robe, then knotted it at the waist and shuffled across the hall.

Night shadows streaked the walls, then suddenly the silhouette of a man bled into view, and her heart pounded. He was in the nursery, leaning over the crib.

Panic shot through her. He was going to take Ryan!

Lunging into the room, she shouted at him to stop, but he scooped up the baby and turned toward her. He wore all black and a ski mask, the only visible part of him was his eyes. Dark eyes that bored into her like lasers.

"Put him down," Brianna said. "Please just leave him alone. He's just a baby…."

He stalked toward her, his hulking form menacing as

he shoved her aside. She grabbed his arm to stop him and get Ryan, but he swung his fist up and slammed it into her face. Her head snapped back, but she sucked in a sharp breath, terror streaking through her as she ran after him.

He raced toward the stairs, and she clawed at his back and shoulders, but he jerked her arm and flung her down the steps. She hit the wall, bounced over the ridges of the staircase and landed in a puddle at the bottom of the steps, the room spinning.

Clutching the baby to him, he vaulted over her. Panicked, she grabbed wildly at his ankle, determined not to let him escape.

"Let go, you bitch." With a snarl, he swung his foot back and slammed it into her nose. Blood spurted, pain rocked through her and the room swirled.

Choking on a sob, she struggled to crawl after him. But he kicked her again, and she lost the battle and collapsed into the darkness.

Her last thought before she passed out was filled with pure terror—she'd just lost Natalie's son.

Chapter Two

Derrick jerked awake, sweating and panting for breath.
Images of that last case had haunted him all night. He
could still see that tiny grave, hear the father's choked
cry, the mother's scream of denial.

That dream had blended into another—memories of
his own father tormenting him as a kid, beating him to
a bloody pulp, making him feel worthless.

He stood, wiped the sweat from his brow and went
to the window. Daylight was barely dawning yet it was
always night in his mind, night filled with dark thoughts
of that case and the mess he'd made of it.

All because he'd let his past get in the way. Let
himself believe the mother's story that the kid's father
was abusing him. Easy to believe. It happened every day.

But in the end, he'd been wrong. The mother had
been the abuser.

Her tears had fooled him.

Never again.

He had to stay detached.

The snow dotting the tree branches reminded him of

Brianna holding that baby at the graveyard the night before. Of the question nagging at him.

Could that little boy be his son?

Hell, if he is, he's probably better off without you. What do you know about fatherhood?

Zilch. Except that he didn't want to be like his old man. And he didn't want some kid thinking he'd deserted him, either.

What kind of mental scars would that give him?

Hissing in frustration, he strode to the bathroom, splashed cold water on his face and stared at himself in the mirror. His eyes looked bloodshot, worry lines fanning around his mouth, the remnants of the nightmares still in his gaunt expression.

No, if that baby was his, he wouldn't hurt him like his father had hurt him.

Dammit. He'd find a way to be the man, the father, the kid deserved, even if he had to take lessons to do it.

And damn Brianna. If she knew the baby was his son, why hadn't she contacted him and told him?

Another woman—another deception. It seemed to be par for the course. Women liked to play games. But he was no player.

He took a quick shower and dressed, then grabbed his weapon and shoved it into the waistband of his jeans. As he went out the door, he tugged on his jacket and slogged out through the snow. A glance at his watch told him it was only 6:00 a.m. Brianna might not be up. Then again, babies awakened early, didn't they?

The snow flurries were dwindling, yet the spiny branches of the trees were coated in white, and dark storm clouds hung heavy in the sky. Gears ground as he chugged up the mountain road toward Brianna's, grateful he'd had snow chains put on the Jeep. The winter wind whistled through the car as he parked in her drive. Squinting through the fog at the small log cabin, he frowned as he noticed her front door stood ajar.

Why would her door be open in cold weather?

Instincts honed from years on the job kicked in, and he removed his gun and climbed out, his gaze scanning her property as he slowly inched toward the porch.

He didn't see anyone lurking around, but still kept his eyes peeled as he neared the front door. A glance inside made his stomach knot.

Brianna was lying on the floor at the bottom of the steps unmoving.

Good God, what had happened?

Adrenaline kicked in as he ran toward her and knelt to check for a pulse. His own clamored as he waited.

A second later, he exhaled in relief. She was breathing.

He placed his gun on the floor beside him, pulled his cell phone from inside his jacket and punched 9-1-1.

"This is Derrick McKinney," he told the operator. "Send an ambulance to Brianna Honeycutt's house. She's unconscious and it looks like she took a fall."

"I'll get an ambulance out there right away," the operator said, then asked for the address.

Derrick gave her directions, then snapped his phone closed, and brushed Brianna's hair from her cheek. "Brianna, can you hear me?" He gently shook her, turning her face sideways to check her injuries.

The bruises on her face made his gut clench.

She hadn't just fallen. Someone had hit her.

Anger churned in his gut, then panic slammed into him. The house was quiet. Too quiet?

Where was the baby?

His heart pounded as he vaulted to his feet and searched the downstairs, then raced up the steps. He spotted Brianna's bedroom on the left, then a guest room across the hall with a crib inside. He hadn't prayed in ages, but he said a silent prayer that the baby was safely asleep in the crib.

But when he looked inside, the baby was gone.

THE SOUND OF A MAN'S GRUFF voice penetrated the fog enveloping Brianna, but a screeching sound trilled in the distance, compounding the pain hammering in her head.

"Brianna, can you hear me?" Soft fingers stroked her cheek. "It's Derrick McKinney. I need you to wake up and talk to me."

She moaned, but slowly roused, and tried to open her eyes. Where was she? What had happened?

"Brianna," he said a little more harshly. "Please. I need you to talk to me."

Panic and fear pummeled her as reality returned. Oh, God…the baby.

"Ryan…" Tears choked her, and she pushed at the floor with her hands, desperate to get up. "The baby…a man…he broke in and took him." The room swirled as she lifted her head, and pain rocked through her again, sending nausea in waves.

"Easy," Derrick urged. "You'd better lie flat until the EMTs get here. You might have a head injury."

"No, I'm okay." She had to drag in a breath to stem the nausea. The room twirled, and she closed her eyes and willed herself not to get sick on him. "Just help me to the couch."

He eased her onto the sofa, then knelt beside her. "Tell me where it hurts," he said.

"I'll be fine," she claimed through gritted teeth, "but he took Ryan." She clutched his arm with an iron grip. "You have to find him, Derrick. You have to."

"I will," he declared softly. "Just tell me what happened. What do you remember?"

She massaged her temple, struggling to recall the details. "I put Ryan to bed after I got home and then went to bed myself. Later, I heard him crying, and went to the nursery, but a man was standing over the crib. Then he grabbed Ryan and started to leave."

"Did you see his face?"

She shook her head. "No, it was so dark, and he was dressed in all black and wearing a ski mask. The only thing I saw was his eyes." A shiver rippled through her, and she slowly sat up. "He had cold, mean eyes."

He stroked her arm as if to calm her. "Then what happened?"

"I tried to stop him, but he hit me, so I ran after him. I caught his arm on the steps, but he threw me down them. Then he ran by me on the stairs." Tears leaked from her eyes and rolled on her cheeks. "I grabbed his ankle, but he kicked me in the face and chest. I was dizzy but I tried to get to him, but he kicked me again and I must have passed out."

She dropped her face into her hands. "Oh, God, Derrick...Ryan is gone and it's all my fault."

DERRICK TRIED TO STEEL HIMSELF against the torment in Brianna's voice, but if there was one emotion he understood, it was guilt. And hers was genuine. No act.

Her sobs tore at him, and he couldn't resist. He pulled her into his arms and held her. It was a cop thing to do, a human comforting another. He'd done it a thousand times on a case.

But never had the person's pain made him ache inside like a knife had ripped open his heart.

And never had he felt so connected with anyone in his life.

The thought scared the crap out of him.

The connection had to do with the missing baby— the baby he thought might be his.

Grasping onto that reality, he gently lifted her away from him. "Brianna, I have to call the sheriff."

"What time is it?" she whispered.

His expression turned grim. "A little after 6:00 a.m. What time did you wake up and hear the baby crying?"

She swiped at the tears streaking her pale, bruised cheeks. "I'm not sure, maybe four, four-thirty."

A siren wailed outside. About damn time, Derrick thought. She could have died before help arrived. If he hadn't stopped by, she might have been lying there for hours.

He stood and reached for his phone. "I'll meet them and call the sheriff. We need to issue an Amber Alert."

"Yes, of course." She clutched his hand. "Please, Derrick. We have to act fast." She caught her lip with her teeth on another sob. He wanted to console her again, but time was of the essence.

She leaned back against the sofa looking stricken as he hurried to meet the ambulance. The paramedics jumped from the vehicle, and walked toward him.

"We got a 9-1-1 call."

His training kicked in. "Yes. Brianna Honeycutt was attacked by an intruder during a baby kidnapping. The perpetrator knocked her unconscious before he escaped. She's awake now, but probably has a concussion. And she may be going into shock."

The medic in the lead nodded. "And you are, sir?"

He produced the ID that Gage had given him. "Guardian Angel Investigations. Before that, I was with the Raleigh P.D., Special Victims Unit."

The medic nodded. "We'll check her out and prepare to transport her to the hospital for tests and observation."

"Thanks. I'll call the local authorities to report the kidnapping." He breathed in the early morning cold air, needing to clear his head as he punched in the sheriff's number. On instinct, he'd immediately programmed into his phone the pertinent numbers he'd need in the area. He'd done his homework, too, and knew that Beau Cramer had taken over as sheriff after Charlie Driscill had resigned. He didn't know the full story there, but he would find out. Driscill's resignation had something to do with Gage and his wife Leah, but he hadn't pushed yet. But if it pertained to a case, he would.

Friends with Gage or not.

"Sheriff Cramer."

"Sheriff, this is Derrick McKinney of Guardian Angel Investigations. I'm with Brianna Honeycutt at her house. You need to get out here. She was attacked, and the baby she adopted was kidnapped."

"I'll be right there."

"Thanks." Derrick phoned GAI to inform Levi he had a case, then snapped his phone shut, and went back inside to check on Brianna. Hopefully, they hadn't wasted too much time while she was unconscious.

Every second, every minute counted.

And every one that passed meant their chances of finding the baby decreased exponentially.

BRIANNA DIDN'T WANT MEDICAL treatment now. She wanted to scream and shout and cry.

She wanted to find her baby.

Pain robbed her breath. She might not have given birth to Ryan, but he was hers.

Only what if Derrick was the father…?

And if he wasn't? What if the birth father found out about Ryan and decided to take him from her? What if he'd been the man in the house?

But why sneak into her house in the middle of the night? Why not come forward and claim his son? DNA tests could have been done….

Unless there was something about him, maybe a

criminal record that would keep a judge from giving him custody? Or if he wanted to get rid of the child.

That horrible possibility sent nausea rolling through her again.

Damn Natalie. Her friend should have told her the truth about the baby's father. And if she was in danger, she should have confided the reason.

"Miss Honeycutt." The medics introduced themselves as Adam and Joe. "We need to check you over."

"I'm okay," Brianna said. "I just need to find my baby."

"One step at a time, ma'am," Adam said. "Let us check your vitals and transport you to the hospital for tests."

"I don't want to go the hospital." Hysteria bubbled in her chest. "My son is missing. I have to find him."

The medic gave her a sympathetic look but coaxed her to lie back down on the sofa. The other one brought an ice pack for her cheek. "I understand, ma'am. But you're injured, and we need to do our jobs. Mr. McKinney has called the sheriff."

Fear overwhelmed her. "But my baby could be anywhere by now...."

The medics exchanged looks, then Adam strapped on a blood pressure cuff while Joe listened to her heart. Frustration knifed through her, but she finally conceded and let them do their jobs.

Another siren wailed in the distance, and Derrick jogged outside to meet the sheriff. By the time they came inside, the medics were insisting that Brianna go to the hospital.

She gave Derrick a determined look. "I'll sign a release. I refuse to go the hospital."

Derrick's dark gaze met hers while Sheriff Cramer folded his arms. Cramer was shorter than Derrick, and stockier. The last time she'd seen him had been at Natalie's funeral where he'd seemed quiet and withdrawn.

"Brianna, are you all right?"

"No," she responded. "Someone kidnapped Ryan."

"We want to take her for tests," the medic explained. "She probably has a concussion and may have some cracked ribs."

"No. The only thing they'll do for a concussion is to tell me to rest," Brianna said. "I'm not going to the hospital."

"Brianna," Derrick urged.

She threw up a warning hand, cutting him off. "What I need," she declared firmly, "is to find Ryan. Now let's stop wasting time and do it."

The medics exchanged frustrated looks, but Derrick finally nodded. "I'll bring her in later if I think she needs it. You guys can go now."

She signed the release form and sighed in relief as they left. Her head and ribs were the least of her problems. The pain in her heart was robbing her breath.

Sheriff Cramer sat down in the club chair beside the couch. "Tell me what happened."

Brianna repeated the story, this time on autopilot.

"We'll find the baby," he assured her. "I've already issued an Amber Alert. Can you describe your attacker?"

She shook her head. "Not really. He was medium height, beefy, wore dark clothes and a ski mask."

"Did he say anything?"

She pinched the bridge of her nose. "Let go, you bitch."

"That's it?"

"Yes."

"Did you see what kind of car he was driving?"

"No," she whispered. "He broke in while I was asleep. I chased him down the steps but he knocked me out. I never made it outside." She drew in a deep breath. "Why would someone take Ryan? I don't have any money."

"How about the baby's father?" Cramer asked.

Brianna's gaze shot to Derrick. "I'm not sure who he is."

"But he could have come after the baby."

She shrugged. "It's possible."

"The baby might be mine," Derrick said, his jaw tight. "I want to run a DNA test."

Cramer's brows shot up in surprise. "You might be the baby's father?"

Derrick gave a clipped nod. "You need a crime unit out here to check for forensics. Maybe this guy left a stray hair or fiber or a print."

"He wore gloves," Brianna said, despair weighing on her.

"I'll get GAI to set up a trace on the phones," Derrick commented. "In case the kidnapper calls wanting a ransom."

Beau stood. "This is my town, McKinney. I'll run the case."

"I don't intend to get into a pissing contest with you," Derrick countered. Good God, the man was years younger than him and probably green when it came to this type of work. "Finding missing children is my specialty, Cramer. It's what I did in Raleigh, it's what I'm doing at Guardian Angel Investigations now."

Cramer puffed up his chest. "I can handle it."

Derrick grunted. "You've only been sheriff, what— three or four months? Have you ever worked a child abduction?"

Cramer gritted his teeth. "No, but I'm perfectly capable."

"Then you'll let me work with you," Derrick said in a tone that brooked no argument.

Cramer and Derrick stared at each other for a tense moment, but finally Cramer must have realized the futility in arguing and excused himself to call the crime unit.

Derrick joined Brianna on the couch. "Brianna, we have to examine all possibilities. Finding out who Ryan's father is may be the key."

"There's a baby brush upstairs," she said, knotting her hands.

He touched her hand to calm her. "I'll get it in a minute. But I need to ask you something else. Is there anyone in town who might want to hurt you by taking Ryan? Do you have any enemies?"

Her first instinct was to say no. But the memory of her encounter with Dana Phillips flashed back, and her gut clenched.

"You thought of someone, didn't you?" Derrick asked.

Brianna hesitated. She hated to throw suspicion on one of her clients, especially one so vulnerable and desperate for a child. But that desperation could also prove to be a motive.

"Brianna, tell me the truth. Who are you thinking of?"

"This young woman I've been working with," she answered quietly. "She and her husband have been trying to adopt, but we haven't found a baby for them."

"You think she might have kidnapped Ryan?"

"I don't know," Brianna replied. "I hate to accuse her and her husband. I'm supposed to be helping them."

Derrick gripped her arms. "Listen to me. If they're innocent, you can apologize. But every second we hesitate gives the kidnapper a chance to get farther away."

She bit her lip but nodded. "Dana was upset with me yesterday. She wanted me to give her custody of Ryan. She said two parents were better than one."

Derrick shot up from the couch. "Give me their names and address."

Brianna scribbled down the information, her pulse racing. If the Phillips couple had taken Ryan, at least she knew he was safe, that they wouldn't hurt him.

But if they hadn't, then some madman might have Ryan.

And there was no telling what he might do.

Chapter Three

Derrick jogged up the stairs, found the baby brush, plucked a couple of strands of hair from it and bagged it to send to the lab.

He found a Q-tip in the bathroom, swabbed his mouth and placed the swab in another bag, hurried down the steps, then stopped in front of Brianna. "I'm going to call the tech specialist at GAI and place a trace on your home phone, and have him forward any calls to your cell as well so we're not stuck here waiting."

She nodded and gave him her home and cell numbers, then he stepped outside to meet the sheriff. "Cramer, will you send this to the lab with the CSI team and have them run the DNA for a paternity test?"

Cramer frowned but agreed. "Where are you going, McKinney?"

Derrick shoved his hands in the pockets of his leather bomber jacket. "I just got into town. I have a couple of things to take care of."

Cramer narrowed his eyes. "What kind of things?"

Derrick debated whether to tell him the truth. But if

the sheriff showed up at the Phillipses' door, they might panic and run. Unless they'd already left town…

He'd check them out on his own.

"I have to meet my boss before he leaves town. And I'm going to get a trace put on Brianna's phone, and have her calls forwarded to her cell in case the kidnapper calls."

"You're working for Gage McDermont?"

Derrick nodded. "He and Leah are going on a second honeymoon. I need to fill him in on what's happened."

"You're not holding out on me, are you?"

"Of course not. I wouldn't do anything to jeopardize this case."

"Did Brianna give you some idea who might have kidnapped the baby?" Cramer asked.

He shook his head. "No. What's your next move?"

Cramer glanced at the woods. "I'll call in some deputies from the county and form a search party to check any abandoned houses and cabins in the woods."

Derrick nodded. "I'll ask Brock Running Bear from GAI to help with the search. Check the hotels, too."

Cramer pulled at his chin. "I planned to."

Derrick strode to his car, climbed in and started the engine. He hated to leave Brianna alone, but she should be safe with the sheriff there. And the clock was ticking. He quickly called GAI. Ben agreed to set up the trace and have Brock join the search parties.

Early morning sunlight filtered through the trees, glistening off the snowpacked ground and mountaintops as he drove toward town. The Phillips couple lived in a small ranch in one of the older subdivisions on the edge of Sanctuary, a redbrick with neatly trimmed boxwoods lining the front. A fenced-in yard encased the back. He checked for a dog, but didn't hear one barking or see an animal as he glanced around the corner of the house.

The lights were off, and he wondered if the Phillipses were still in bed, or if they'd already left for work. Suddenly a light flicked on at the end of the house in the front room, and he stepped to the side to look inside, and saw a man in the kitchen.

He debated on whether to confront the couple, or stake them out, and decided on the latter. He crept back to his car and slipped inside so he could watch the front.

If they exited with the baby, he'd catch them red-handed.

BRIANNA SAID A SILENT PRAYER that the Phillips couple had Ryan. At least she would know that he was safe, not with some dangerous child molester or someone wanting money.

Money she didn't have.

And if Derrick wasn't Ryan's father, who was? Natalie hadn't mentioned being involved with anyone else. Although Natalie had always been freer about sleeping around than she was.

In fact, she was shocked when Natalie turned up pregnant. Her friend had always been careful and insisted she didn't want to settle down.

Sheriff Cramer strode back downstairs. He'd been showing the CSI team the nursery. They were dusting for prints and combing the rooms and stairs for evidence.

Arms folded, he crossed the room to her. She was still

resting on the couch and pulled her robe tighter around her, anxious for the men to leave so she could shower and dress. Maybe by then, Derrick would call.

Or return with Ryan.

"Brianna, I know McKinney asked you this, but can you think of anyone who'd want to kidnap the baby?"

She shook her head. Natalie had seemed worried at the hospital. But maybe she'd imagined that fear.

"You don't happen to have some money stowed away somewhere? Maybe an inheritance?"

A sarcastic laugh escaped her. "No, I grew up at Magnolia Manor," she said. "Mother left me there when I was seven. Never knew my father." She fiddled with the strap of her robe. "And if I did have money, I'd donate it to Magnolia Manor to help the other needy kids."

"Do you have a picture of the baby? I'll need it for the media and so I can fax it to the Web site for the National Center for Missing & Exploited Children."

She'd taken dozens in the last six weeks. Had even bought a new digital camera so she could download them to her computer.

"Yes." She pushed herself up. "Let me get you one."

She walked over to the table, then glanced at the assortment of photographs. First the one from the hospital the night Ryan had been born. Another photo two weeks later in a sailor's outfit. Another the next week in a baseball hat. But her gaze rested on the photo she'd snapped the week before.

She'd propped Ryan up in the infant seat, and dressed him in a soft blue terry cloth sleeper. The picture showed his pale blond hair, his toothless grin and his chubby cheeks. He'd already changed from birth. In fact, he seemed to change every day.

Grief assailed her. Natalie was missing it all. But she'd trusted Brianna to care for him, and she'd let her down. What would happen if they didn't find Ryan soon?

He might change so much she wouldn't even recognize him….

Swiping at fresh tears, she handed the picture to the sheriff. "Here, this one is the most recent."

"I'll get it sent ASAP." He offered her a tight smile. "Try to hang in there, Brianna. I'll send a deputy here to watch the house if you want."

She shook her head then hugged her arms around herself. "No, I'm fine. Besides, if that man had wanted to kill me, he would have. He obviously just wanted the baby."

"Now we just have to figure out the reason," the sheriff said. "And wait for a ransom call."

Brianna twisted her hands together, praying the kidnapper would phone. Or that Derrick found Ryan first. That he brought him back safely and this nightmare would end.

CAREFUL NOT TO LET THE neighbors see him, Derrick slumped in the seat as two of them pulled from their driveways and passed his car.

The cold seeped through him, but he'd long ago grown used to stakeouts. He just wished he'd brought a thermos of coffee to warm his hands and stave off the exhaustion weighing on him from lack of sleep.

Finally the front door of the Phillipses' house opened, and a man dressed in jeans and work boots carrying a hard hat stepped out. A woman stood behind him in a thick bathrobe, tears streaming down her face. The man shouted something he couldn't distinguish, then turned and stormed toward his car. When he climbed inside, he slammed the door and took off, speeding from the drive as if he wanted to escape. The woman slammed the house door, then disappeared inside.

Derrick frowned. It appeared the couple was having marital problems. Maybe arguing over whether or not they should have kidnapped the baby?

If they had, why would they stay in town? Why wouldn't they have disappeared?

They would have to know that Brianna would confide about her altercation with them and the sheriff would check them out.

He needed to talk to the husband alone, but first he wanted to see if the baby was inside, so he remained parked, watching. A half hour later, the woman appeared at the door again, this time dressed and wearing a long black coat. The snowfall had ceased, but the driveway had accumulated a couple of inches of snow, so she slowly picked her way to the car.

She wasn't carrying a baby, and he didn't see a child's seat in the car, either.

Maybe she had a sitter inside?

Or what if she had hired someone to kidnap the baby? She could be meeting with him later to pick up Ryan.

Although at the moment, she didn't have a diaper bag or any supplies with her. And she didn't bring a suitcase, so she wasn't leaving town.

She might be desperate, but she probably knew

Brianna would send the sheriff to her door, so decided to lay low and wait until the dust settled, then connect with the kidnapper afterward. That would be the smart thing to do.

He kept his head down while she veered onto the street and waited until her car had cleared the corner. Then he slipped from his vehicle, crept along the side of the house to the back. Beside the stoop, he found a laundry room window, jimmied it open and climbed inside.

Instincts alert, he hesitated in the doorway joining the laundry room to the kitchen, listening to make sure no one was inside.

But an ominous silence filled the house.

He combed through the kitchen, searched the cabinets to see if the Phillipses had stocked up on baby formula, but found nothing. In the same vein of thinking, he checked the living room, bathroom and two bedrooms—looking for baby paraphernalia, diapers and baby toys—and found a book of baby names where several had been circled. A white bassinet sat against the wall, but it was empty except for a stuffed lamb lying inside.

Was this bassinet for Ryan?

He needed to talk to the couple. But first he rushed to the desk and searched their computer and business records for any financials indicating they'd hired someone to kidnap Ryan.

What he was doing was illegal, but desperate times called for desperate measures.

Too often he'd had to wait on warrants and the perp had escaped. It was damn nice not to have to play by the rules.

AS SOON AS THE SHERIFF AND crime unit left, Brianna phoned her office, explained what had happened, and arranged for another social worker to take over her workload until Ryan was found. Then she dragged herself into the shower and washed off the stench of her attacker. She shampooed and dried her hair, then dressed in jeans and a thick sweater, her heart aching as she glanced at the empty crib.

The first week after Natalie had died, she'd been too grief-stricken to do anything but buy the essentials. A baby bed, a cradle for the downstairs, car seat, bottles, diapers, toys and baby clothes. When she'd cleaned out Natalie's apartment, she'd found a few onesies and baby clothes Natalie had already purchased along with an infant bathtub, diaper bag and baby book.

Brianna hadn't been able to open the baby book yet.

Still, she'd vowed to Natalie that her son would know how much she'd loved him.

What if she never got the chance?

Pain gnawed at her insides, but she willed herself to be strong. Derrick and the sheriff would find Ryan. She couldn't, *wouldn't* allow herself to believe anything else.

And she had to admit that it was comforting to have Derrick working on the case.

By the time she descended the steps, she heard a pounding on the door and Derrick calling her name. She rushed to let him in, but disappointment filled her when she saw the bleak expression on his face.

"What happened?"

Snowflakes swirled with the wind, and he quickly

stepped inside, stomped his boots on the mat and closed the door. "I didn't talk to the Phillips couple."

"Why not?"

He ushered her into the living room. "I wanted to watch them first. To see if they had the baby. They didn't."

Brianna's stomach caved. "If they don't have him, who does? Some child predator? Someone who wants money that I don't have?" She hadn't realized how much she'd banked her hopes on the fact that Dana had Ryan and was taking good care of him.

That he wasn't in danger from a crazed, cold-blooded killer who might take money, then kill him anyway.

Derrick stroked her arms. "Listen Brianna, I've worked these cases before. If they kidnapped Ryan, they obviously hired someone else to the job which means they're planning to meet him later. I waited until both of them left home, then searched the house."

Her hopes skyrocketed. "What did you find? Evidence they'd paid someone or were preparing for Ryan?"

He gave a noncommittal shrug. "Not exactly. There is a crib in the house, and a book of baby names. But no formula, diapers or supplies to indicate they were expecting a baby right away. And their financial records didn't indicate a recent large withdrawal as if they'd paid a kidnapper."

She sank onto the sofa. "But they could be meeting the kidnapper out of town?"

"It's possible, although neither left with a suitcase. If they're smart though, they'll probably wait a few days before making the connection."

She grabbed his arm, adrenaline kicking in. "Then

we have to talk to them now. Dana is emotional. Maybe she'll break down and tell me where he is."

Derrick's look turned skeptical, but they had no other leads and she had to do something. "Please, Derrick. I know Dana is on the edge. She wants a baby so badly she's unstable. Maybe if I talk to her, woman to woman, she'll open up." Either that, or the woman would hate her.

But at this point, she didn't care. All that mattered was finding little Ryan. Because if Dana didn't have him, someone else did.

And for once in her life, she couldn't waste time playing nice.

HE CURSED AT THE SOUND OF THE baby crying from the backseat. "Hush up, kid. I'll get you out soon."

He swung the car into the motel parking lot, circled around to the backseat and unbuckled the kid, then picked him up. The baby's cries escalated to a blazing crescendo, and he jiggled him up and down. "I can't believe I'm doing this," he muttered. "It's so not worth the cash."

With the key he'd pocketed earlier, he strode down the row of rooms, and let himself inside.

Candy, his girlfriend, lay stretched out on the bed, blowing at her hot red fingernails reading a magazine. When she looked up at the screaming infant, she pursed her lips. "I can't believe you brought the brat here."

"You have to take care of him, sugar, until we can drop him off."

"You're kidding, right?" She stood, hands on voluptuous hips. "I don't know anything about taking care of a baby."

"Then learn." He gestured toward the bag of baby supplies he'd stowed earlier. "Get him a bottle and take him. I gotta make a call."

She frowned and made a pouty look, but did as he said.

Shoulders straightening, he stepped outside with his phone and punched in the number. "I have the baby. It's done."

"And Brianna Honeycutt?"

"She woke up and tried to stop me. I threw her down the stairs, but she's alive."

"Damn. If she keeps asking questions, we'll have to get rid of her, too."

"You have a plan?"

"Yeah. We'll kill her, then fake a suicide note where she confesses that she dropped the baby at an orphanage because she couldn't handle the kid."

"And she cried kidnapping to throw suspicion from herself?"

"Exactly."

Laughter boomed from his chest. That sounded like a plan that would work. They'd drop the kid, get rid of the problematic woman, take their money and run.

Chapter Four

"Where does Dana Phillips work?" Derrick asked.

"She's a receptionist at the insurance office in town." Brianna stewed over whether she believed the young couple would resort to kidnapping. "And Robert is the head of the construction team building those new cabins on the east side of town."

"They were arguing when he left the house," Derrick said. "Maybe their fight had to do with the baby."

"Or it's possible it had nothing to do with this and the kidnapper is long gone."

"There hasn't been a call?" Derrick asked.

Brianna shook her head. "No. I can't figure out what the kidnapper wants."

Derrick's silence added to the anxiety knotting her insides. "I'll talk to Dana."

"I'm going with you," Brianna stated.

He paused, his look filled with concern. "Are you sure you're up to that, Brianna? You have a concussion, and the medic said you probably cracked some ribs."

"I'll be fine," she said. "I can't just sit here and wait, Derrick. I'm going crazy."

"All right. But if you start to feel bad, let me know."

Brianna agreed, grabbed her coat and purse, and they hurried to his Jeep. The temperature had dropped, and she burrowed in her coat, but the chill inside her had nothing to do with the weather. Images of Ryan crying, cold, in the hands of a madman taunted her.

Christmas lights and decorations glittered in town, decorative snowflakes and wreaths adorning the storefront windows, and red bows had been tacked on every streetlamp and sign. It would be a picture perfect Christmas with the snow blanketing the town.

Except that a kidnapper had escaped and a tiny little baby was missing. Her son.

"There's the insurance office," Brianna said.

Derrick swung the vehicle into a parking space in the square, jumped out and circled to the passenger's side to help her, but Brianna was already pushing open the door and getting out. He took her arm to steady her as they dodged an icy patch on the sidewalk, and climbed the two steps to the office door. A Santa had been painted on the window, advertising that he would bring savings in your stocking with a life insurance plan.

Derrick opened the door, and Brianna spotted Dana sitting at the front desk typing on the computer. When Dana saw Derrick, a wariness darkened her expression.

A frisson of guilt attacked Brianna. If Dana hadn't kidnapped Ryan, accusing her was cruel. But Dana was their only viable suspect right now.

"Brianna, what are you doing here?" Dana asked.

"I have to talk to you." Brianna lowered her voice. "Ryan has been kidnapped, Dana."

Dana's eyes widened. "What?"

Brianna gestured to the bruises on her face. "Someone broke into my house early this morning, knocked me unconscious, then took the baby."

The color drained from Dana's face. "My God, that's horrible. Do you know who did it?"

For a brief moment, Dana stood as if to console Brianna, then her expression changed as if she realized the reason for their visit. "You can't think that I had something to do with this?"

Derrick cleared his throat. "Mrs. Phillips, my name is Derrick McKinney. I'm with Guardian Angel Investigations and I'm trying to find the baby. If you know something, please tell us now."

"*If* I know something," Dana echoed shrilly. Tears shimmered in her eyes. "I can't believe you'd come here like this, Brianna. First of all, you were supposed to help me adopt a baby, then you adopt the first infant that comes along, and now you have the audacity to accuse me of kidnapping."

"Please, Dana," Brianna pleaded. "I'm just trying to find Ryan. I…don't know where to turn. You were really upset with me yesterday and you said you wanted Ryan."

"I did," Dana said. "And if you find him, I still think he'd be better off with me and Robert. After all, you had him and you let someone take him from your home. What kind of mother are you?"

BRIANNA SHUDDERED AS IF SHE'D been slapped. Derrick gritted his teeth at Dana's statement, his suspicious nature kicking in. Could she have arranged to have the baby kidnapped to make Brianna look like a bad mother to give her ammunition for a custody case?

That sounded drastic, but the young woman didn't actually seem stable. Had her obsession with wanting a child pushed her over the line?

"Mrs. Phillips, we're not accusing you of anything," Derrick explained. "But if you do know who kidnapped the baby, it would be in your best interests to tell the truth. Give him back, and we can make a deal not to press charges."

"I didn't take the baby," Dana declared, her voice filled with fury. "Now get out of my office and don't come back."

Derrick gripped Brianna by the arm, then tossed his business card on the woman's desk. "Call me if there's any way you can help us."

He led Brianna out into the cold, trying to decide his next move.

"She hates me now," Brianna said in a pained voice.

"She'll get over it."

"But she's right. I let Natalie and Ryan down." She turned to search the streets, then looked toward the steep mountain ridges. "What if he's out there somewhere with a crazy man, someone who won't take care of him?"

"Don't go there, Brianna, it won't do any good." He ushered her to the car, and they settled inside. She huddled in her coat, and he started the car and flipped up the heater. "The sheriff is organizing a search party for the mountains. If the kidnapper is holed up around here somewhere, we'll find him."

"And what if he's long gone?"

"Then the Amber Alert should help." He reached over and squeezed her hand.

"So what do we do now? Just wait?"

"Let's talk to Dana's husband. Maybe he can shed some light on the truth."

Brianna clasped her hands in her lap as he drove to the construction site. The crew had temporarily ceased work due to the snowstorm, but they found Robert Phillips in the office of an on-site trailer. Through the window, Derrick noticed Phillips pacing. He was obviously agitated.

Derrick knocked and opened the door before the man could answer. When Phillips saw them enter, he frowned. "I'll call you later, Dana," he said. "Try to calm down."

He snapped his phone closed, then shoved his hand through his hair. "I just talked to Dana. She's hysterical."

"I'm sorry," Brianna apologized. "I…don't know what to say, but someone kidnapped Ryan last night, Robert, and I didn't know where to turn."

"You thought Dana arranged to have him kidnapped?"

Brianna bit her lip, but Derrick spoke up. "We have to explore all possibilities. Since Brianna hasn't received a ransom call, and has no major assets to invite ransom, we have to look at other options."

"And my wife is desperate for a baby, so you came to her first?" Anger laced Phillips's voice, but there was a twinge of understanding—as if he recognized their point.

Derrick shrugged. "She did have an altercation with Brianna yesterday morning."

"I know." Phillips scrubbed his hand over the slight beard on his chin. "Dana has been distraught and overly emotional lately. She's obsessed with getting a baby." A look of anguish flashed in his eyes. "It's tearing our marriage apart." The big guy slumped down in his chair with a heavy sigh. "We even argued this morning because I told her I had second thoughts about adopting. I mean I want a kid, but I can be happy with just her and me. But Dana…"

"She needs counseling," Brianna said.

He leaned his forehead on his hand. "I tried to talk her into counseling, too, but she got mad and accused me of not wanting a child."

"You don't think she took the baby, do you?" Brianna asked.

Again, he looked pained, even torn, but finally he shook his head. "No. She may be desperate, and I know she lashed out at you, but she'd never steal a child."

"She didn't happen to withdraw any money lately?" Derrick asked.

"No."

"Will you check your account?" Derrick insisted.

Phillips's mouth tightened as he clicked a few keys on the computer, then pulled up his bank account. He studied it for a moment, then angled his head toward them. "Take a look yourself. There are no cash withdrawals, and the only checks are for the house, bills and groceries."

Derrick believed the guy, but gave the screen a perfunctory glance just to make certain he wasn't covering for his wife. "How about her family? Would Dana have access to money from them?"

"She and her family don't get along," Phillips said. "They live somewhere up north. She'd never go to them for help or tell them about our problems having a child."

With a weary sigh, Phillips stood. "Listen, I am sorry about the baby, Brianna. You have been wonderful to us. If y'all are organizing a search party, I'd be glad to help. I know these mountains like the back of my hand. And when I was looking for sites for this project, I found a few abandoned cabins someone could use to hide out in."

Brianna sighed softly, obviously touched. "Thank you, Robert. I appreciate that."

For a moment, Derrick hesitated, his suspicious nature kicking in. Could the young man be offering help to lead them astray?

But barring his last case, the mistake with the woman, he was usually a good judge of character, and everything about the man's frustration with his wife and his apology to Brianna rang true.

"If you really mean that," Derrick commented, "check with the sheriff. He's arranging a team, and with your knowledge of the area and buildings, you could be of value."

Phillips reached for his coat. "I'll go see the sheriff now."

They all walked out together, and Brianna thanked the man then climbed in the car. Brianna's shoulders slumped with fatigue and stress, while tension thrummed through Derrick's body.

The thought of Ryan being in danger knotted his insides. He had to find him.

He couldn't live with himself if he didn't.

"What do we do now?" Brianna asked.

His mind ticked over other cases, and he had a thought. "Let me do some digging around at the hospital. See if anyone lost a baby there recently."

"Nobody is going to release medical records," Brianna said. "Not with the strict privacy laws now."

True. But not being with the bureau or the sheriff might work to their advantage.

"Do you have any contacts at the hospital?" he asked. "Maybe a friend who works there?"

Brianna hesitated. "Actually Sherry Ann Simmons is a nurse on the labor and delivery unit. She came to the waiting room to console me the night Natalie died."

A muscle jumped in his cheek. "Then let's go see Sherry Ann."

BRIANNA STRUGGLED TO HOLD ONTO hope as they drove to the hospital. She hated the confrontation with Dana, and prayed she hadn't pushed the young woman over the edge. Derrick parked, and Brianna climbed from the seat, sucking in a sharp breath as pain ricocheted through her ribs. Her head was beginning to throb again, and her muscles ached from her fall down the stairs.

Derrick took her arm to help her along the icy pathway, and she forced a smile between clenched teeth.

"I can tell you're hurting, Bri," he said quietly. "I can take you home anytime."

"No." Panic stabbed at her. She didn't want to be alone, not with her guilt, her worries and her imagination skipping to dark places. Not with the empty silence of the house. "I have to see this through."

A ceiling-high Christmas tree stood in the hospital lobby, bows and garland decorating the walls, another reminder that Christmas would be here in a few days. They rode the elevator to the third floor, and the doors swished open to reveal another glittering tree. Nurses bustled back and forth with their morning chores. A baby cried from down the hall, and orderlies were delivering breakfast trays to the rooms.

Brianna made her way to the nurses' station where a young aide sat filing charts behind the desk.

"Hi, is Sherry Ann Simmons on duty this morning?"

The young girl nodded. "Yes, she just went to help feed the preemies."

"We'll wait then." She and Derrick walked to the nursery window, and paused by the glass partition. Rows of babies in bassinets lined the wall, and in the middle, three infants were in incubators, some sleeping, others crying, while the nurses tended to them.

Derrick made a low throaty sound, and turmoil darkened his brown eyes.

"If Ryan was mine, why didn't Natalie tell me?" he finally asked.

"I don't know," Brianna said. "Maybe she thought you wouldn't care, or that you wouldn't want him. Or maybe she didn't want you to think she was trying to trap you."

His grunt resonated with disbelief.

Then he turned toward her, belligerence in his

stance. "When Natalie died, why didn't you tell me about the baby?"

Brianna sighed. "Derrick, I told you that I didn't know who the father was, not for sure."

"If you had, would you have let me know?"

The question taunted her, digging at her own self-doubt and guilt. She didn't know how to answer. Yet she'd gone all her life without knowing her father and she had no right to deny Ryan his.

"I don't know," she replied honestly. "That was Natalie's decision, not mine."

He gripped her arm. "If he's mine, Brianna, I'm going to be in his life. I'm going to get custody."

Brianna tensed. She didn't want to lose Ryan. But if Derrick discovered she'd faked the paperwork, she would. And she'd lose her job.

She spotted Sherry feeding a newborn and waved, and mouthed that she wanted to see her, and Sherry motioned that she'd be out in a minute.

"Brianna," Derrick began. "Natalie told me that she was seeing someone else the last few months. Do you know who it was?"

Brianna shrugged. "No. But I think he was one of the deputies in the county."

"He could have discovered Ryan was his, and had him kidnapped."

"I thought of that, but why? If he'd wanted Ryan, why not come forward or go through the court?"

"Maybe he has something in his past or his background that would keep him from obtaining custody."

Brianna pursed her lips. "I guess that's possible."

"I need to know who she dated," Derrick declared.

The door squeaked open then, and Sherry stepped into the hallway. She smelled of baby, soft and gooey, and Brianna smiled, remembering the way the young woman had comforted her the night Natalie had died.

"Hi, Brianna, how are you doing?"

"Not very well," Brianna responded. "I don't know if you've seen the news but baby Ryan was kidnapped from my house in the night."

Shock strained Sherry's features. "No, I didn't know."

Derrick introduced himself, and Sherry gave him a curious look. "Miss Simmons, the sheriff has issued an Amber Alert and is organizing a team to search the mountains for the kidnapper. I'm working with Brianna to help find the baby."

"What can I do?" Sherry prodded.

Brianna clutched Sherry's hand. "I know this is asking a lot, but we're investigating the possibility that a desperate woman had the baby kidnapped. Maybe one who wanted to adopt, or someone who recently lost a child."

Sherry's eyes widened. "Bri, you know I want to help you, but I can't violate patient confidentiality."

"So there is someone who comes to mind?" Derrick suggested.

Sherry chewed her lip and averted her eyes, remaining silent as another nurse exited the nursery and passed by.

"We just need a name," Brianna urged. "No one will know that you gave us information, I promise that."

"I'll have to check the files," she said in a hushed whisper. "But yes, last week a woman came in and miscarried. It was her third so far, and the doctor warned her not to try again, that she'd probably never be able to carry a baby to term."

Sympathy welled in Brianna's chest. She'd heard the story before from others who had turned to adoption. Losing the child was emotionally and physically painful enough, but couple that with hormones and the loss of hope, and the woman might have snapped. "She must have been devastated."

"She was," Sherry agreed softly. "You could hear her crying all the way down the hall. And her husband was almost as distraught."

"What is her name?" Derrick asked.

Sherry motioned for them to follow her, and she ducked into an empty office and accessed the computer. A few seconds later, she scribbled a name and address on a sticky note. "Please be gentle," Sherry begged. "This woman is emotionally fragile."

Brianna's chest clenched at Sherry's plea. The last thing she wanted to do was torture another woman, especially after all she'd suffered so far.

But they had to do everything possible to find Ryan.

And this woman might have stolen him to replace the child she couldn't have.

Chapter Five

Hoping the woman who'd miscarried proved to be a lead, Derrick drove through town, then to a complex of duplexes in an older section on the west side. Although the units had been built twenty years before, the brick had held up well and many were decorated for the holidays. The playground to the right was deserted now, but in the warmer weather, he imagined it was packed with kids.

Rhoda Hampton and her husband lived in the unit on the end. Good. Better access to break in if he needed to.

"I really hate to do this," Brianna said. "This woman sounds like she's been through hell already."

Derrick gripped the steering wheel with clenched fingers. "I know, Brianna. But time is important here. We can't afford not to pursue any possibility."

Brianna pulled out her phone and glanced at it before they got out. "I just wish the kidnapper would call. I want to know that Ryan is okay."

So did he. And every minute that passed lessened his chances of finding the baby alive. The very reason he had to steel himself against sympathy for this other woman and do his job.

He glanced at Brianna. The bruises on her face were more stark. Her skin had darkened to a deep purple and yellow in the afternoon sunlight flickering off the snow.

"You can wait here if you want," Derrick offered. "I can handle it."

"No." Brianna opened her own door. "I'm a social worker. Maybe I can make her understand, connect on some level."

They walked up the driveway together, but Derrick kept his eyes peeled in case the woman was watching. The duplex seemed dark though, and no car was in the drive.

Brianna punched the doorbell, but he peeked through the front window for signs of life. No lights inside. No movement or sounds.

Brianna punched the bell again, but no one responded. Derrick motioned that he was going around back, and she followed him to the kitchen door.

It was locked, so he used a credit card, and a second later, opened the door.

She caught his arm. "Derrick, we can't break in."

"Shh." He inched inside, and paused to listen, but a dark silence filled the house as if it had been deserted.

"Stay outside," Derrick ordered.

Brianna hesitated at the doorway, then seemed to change her mind and stepped inside. Afternoon shadows hugged the walls as he studied the kitchen. A half pot of coffee sat on the counter, but it was cold, and dishes crusted with dried food had been left in the sink.

"What are you looking for?" Brianna asked.

"Some sign the couple brought a baby here."

Brianna nodded, watching as he checked the pantry and refrigerator. No baby formula inside. They slowly walked into the den, and his gaze skimmed the room. A worn leather sofa and recliner, TV, magazines scattered across a pine coffee table. No baby furniture.

He inched up the steps, his senses honed in case someone was hiding upstairs or returned. Brianna stepped into the master bedroom while he moved to the guest room to check it out. An iron bed, wooden dresser and rocking chair occupied the room, but he didn't find a baby bed. He quickly searched the closet, the dresser drawers and then headed to the last room.

It was empty, and obviously intended to be the nursery, because it had been painted blue and a train border lined the wall near the ceiling. Apparently that was as far as the couple had gotten with the nursery.

Brianna approached from behind. "Oh, that's so sad. I feel badly for them."

"There's nothing here," he reported. "Did you find anything?"

"I'm not sure," Brianna said. "The dresser drawers were half open as if someone might have pulled clothes from them in a hurry, and the closet door was ajar."

"Any suitcases inside?"

She frowned. "Yes, a big one."

"Might have been a smaller matching one to go with it. Maybe they left town in a hurry." He gestured toward the hall. "Let's check downstairs and see if we find work numbers. I want to know where this couple is."

He let her go first, grimacing as she winced with

every movement and gripped the stair rail to steady herself. "Check that desk in the den and I'll search the kitchen by the phone."

She stopped at the desk and began to rummage through the papers on top. He checked the kitchen counter, then found a basket with a few bills inside, and a business card for Larry Hampton. He grabbed the latest bank statement and stuck it inside his jacket.

"He owns a pesticide company called Bugs Away." Derrick pocketed the card, gestured toward the back door, and they rushed outside and around front to the car.

As he settled in the driver's seat, he scanned the complex, removed his phone and punched in the number for Bugs Away. The phone rang twice, then a woman's voice echoed over the line.

"Bugs Away. How can I help you?"

"Is Larry Hampton in?"

"I'm sorry, sir, but he called yesterday and said he was going to be out of town for a few days. Do you need one of our assistants to come out for an estimate?"

"No, thank you. Did Mr. Hampton say where he was going?"

"No. Would you like us to mail you a brochure?"

"No, thanks. I really need to talk to him and his wife. Do you know where Mrs. Hampton works?"

"She teaches math at the high school. Why? What is this about?"

Derrick didn't bother to reply. He hung up the phone, then called information for the number of the school. The receptionist answered in a cheery voice.

"Sanctuary High. Trudy Leigh speaking."

"Hi, Trudy. I'm the father of a boy in Ms. Hampton's class. Can you tell me if she's at school today? I need to set up a conference."

"Hmm, Ms. Hampton's not here today. In fact, her husband phoned and said there was a family emergency, and she wouldn't be in this week, so we called a substitute. Maybe you can schedule when she returns."

"Yes, thank you." He ended the call, and turned to Brianna, then explained.

"So neither of them showed up at work," Brianna said. "Maybe they just needed some time after the miscarriage."

Derrick gritted his teeth. "Or they might have left town to meet the man who kidnapped Ryan."

And if they had, they probably wouldn't be coming back.

"Maybe we should visit the school and talk to some of the teachers or the principal," Brianna suggested. "One of them might know where the Hamptons have gone."

Derrick grimaced but gave a nod, then ripped open the bank statement he'd confiscated from the couple's house. Brianna leaned sideways to study the posts.

"No large sums of cash," Derrick uttered with a frown. "Unless he went to an ATM and it hasn't shown up yet." He stuffed the statement back into the envelope, then started the car and headed toward the high school.

Ten minutes later, they stood in the front office, talking to a twenty-something secretary named Angie who Brianna knew from high school as well as from prior cases she'd been called to assist with when she'd worked for Division of Family and Children Services.

The receptionist took one look at Brianna and gasped. "My God, Brianna. I heard that you were attacked and someone stole baby Ryan. Are you all right?"

The pros and cons of living in a small town—everyone knew everyone else's business. "No, I'm not," Brianna stressed, her heart in her throat. "And I won't be until I find Ryan."

"I just can't believe it," Angie remarked. "First Natalie dies, and now her baby is kidnapped. Makes me think about that other kidnapping, little Ruby Holden. Why, it was last year about this time."

Derrick cleared his throat and introduced himself, then explained that he worked for GAI. "That's why we're here. We're trying to find out who kidnapped Ryan."

Angie pressed her hand to her chest. "Well, how can I help?"

Brianna lowered her voice. "One of your teachers, Miss Hampton. We heard she had a miscarriage, and that it wasn't her first."

"Yes, that was so sad. She wanted a baby so much, and this was her third try." She leaned forward in a conspiratorial whisper. "She's taking some time off this week. I have a feeling she needed it."

"That's what we heard," Brianna confirmed. "I'm sure she's having a difficult time now, in a vulnerable emotional state."

Angie nodded vehemently. "I was worried that she might have a breakdown. Poor thing." Her mouth quirked sideways in thought. "You know I suggested she talk to you about applying to adopt, but she didn't take it very well. She said she wanted a baby of her own."

"Do you think it's possible she might have changed her mind? That she was desperate enough to hire someone to take Ryan?" Derrick asked.

"Oh, my goodness," Angie said, fiddling with her opal necklace. "You think she kidnapped the baby?"

"I don't know," Brianna admitted. "And I certainly don't want to accuse an already distraught woman who just lost a child of a crime." But if Rhoda Hampton worked with Natalie and had watched her carry her pregnancy to term as an unwed mother, maybe she had decided it wasn't fair, that she should have the child instead of Natalie.

"Still, you can see how it looks," Derrick began. "How we might think that she did. The timing, her emotional state…it all fits."

Angie sank back into the chair behind her desk. "I don't know. I really just don't know."

"Is there anything you can think of that might help us, Angie? Some place Rhoda and her husband might go to get away?"

Angie shrugged. "Not really."

"Any family?"

"His parents are gone. Her mama lives north of here. But she's in a nursing home on the Blue Ridge Parkway so I don't think Mrs. Hampton would go there."

Derrick made a low sound in his throat, and Brianna sensed his frustration. The adjoining office door opened, and Principal Billings walked out.

Brianna smiled at him, and Angie shrugged as he passed, but both waited until he left the office before continuing.

"One more question," Brianna added. "Did Natalie

seem worried or upset about anything the last few weeks before she died?"

Angie pressed both hands to the sides of her face. "She did seem moody and quiet. I assumed it was the hormones talking, or something to do with a student."

Brianna nodded. She'd hoped for more.

She turned to leave, but Derrick spoke up. "Was there anything else that had upset her?"

A blush crept up Angie's freckled skin, and again, she leaned forward as if she thought someone might be privy to their conversation and call her a gossip.

"Well, she and the principal had words about her staying on after she got pregnant, her being an unwed mother and all." She shook her head, her dark hair shifting around her angular face. "He was worried about the parents, that they'd think Natalie wasn't a good role model for the students."

Brianna's mouth tightened. The two-faced bastard. Billings was four years older than her, but she'd heard rumors that he might have attended that party gone awry eight years ago. The party where a bunch of teens got drunk and had sex.

There had been whispers about a date rape drug, but no one had pressed charges, too afraid of recriminations.

Another downside of living in a small town.

"Did she mention anyone she'd been seeing?" Brianna asked.

"No, not to me. But I think that she and the sheriff— well, he was a deputy before Sheriff Driscill retired— they'd hooked up. Don't know if it's true or not, but that's what I heard."

Derrick stiffened beside her, and she tensed.

When Derrick had mentioned he might be Ryan's father, Beau Cramer had never said a word.

Why had he kept the fact that he and Natalie had been involved from them?

"Do you have Mrs. Hampton's cell phone number?" Derrick asked.

Angie shifted nervously.

"Please," Brianna said. "We simply want to talk to her."

Angie relented and checked the files, then gave them the number, along with the husband's cell number, as well.

Just as they stepped into the hallway, Brianna's cell phone jangled in her purse, and she froze. Maybe it was the kidnapper calling to make a deal.

DERRICK TENSED, WATCHING AS Brianna removed her phone and checked the caller ID. Her face paled slightly, and he glanced at the display box over her shoulder.

The sheriff.

He took her arm and guided her to the exit. "Answer it, Bri. Maybe he's found the baby."

Fear clouded her eyes though as she punched the connect button. "Hello."

He drummed his fingers on his leg while she listened. "Yes, Sheriff, we'll be right there."

She snapped the phone closed and turned to him with a pinched look. "He's at the motel on the outside of town. The owner saw the Amber Alert and reported that she saw a man leaving early this morning with a young baby. It might be Ryan."

Chapter Six

Brianna shivered as they stepped out into the cold and rushed to Derrick's Jeep. Hope mingled with anxiety.

If the man at the motel was alone, where was he going with Ryan? Why hadn't he called? Was he meeting the Phillipses or Hamptons to give them the baby?

Derrick fired up the engine and sped away from the school toward the motel. "This might be the lead we're looking for."

"I hope so."

Derrick tried both cell numbers for the Hamptons but neither answered, so he left a message asking them to return his call. Then he phoned Ben and asked him to dig around and see what he could find on the couple, if they owned any vacation property or had relatives that might help them out. Then he dialed Running Deer's phone.

"Any luck on the search in the mountains?"

"Not so far," Running Deer said. "But we've only gotten started."

Derrick thanked him and hung up. Silence stretched between him and Brianna as he maneuvered along the icy road and parked at the motel. The blinking vacancy sign sent rays of light across the white ground, and mud splattered on the sides of the faded concrete made the building look dreary. Barring the sheriff's car and a small sedan, the parking lot was empty.

She and Derrick hurried to the entrance. When she stepped inside, the scent of smoke, sweat and other stale odors engulfed her. This place was cheap, off the road, a stopover for truckers en route to the Blue Ridge Parkway. Most tourists and visitors stayed in the downtown hotel or the Bed & Breakfast on Main Street.

Brianna spotted a short gray-haired woman with leathery skin and cigarette-stained teeth talking to Sheriff Cramer. Derrick crossed the distance over the threadbare carpet with precision. She pressed her hand to her sore rib to stem the ache walking created.

The sheriff gestured to the woman. "This is Henrietta Stoly. She's the one who called about the man."

Brianna introduced herself and Derrick.

"You said there was a man here with a baby?" Derrick asked.

The little woman nodded and gestured toward the photograph of Ryan that Brianna had given him. "I can't be sure it's the same baby. I didn't get a good look at him, but he was wrapped in a blue blanket."

"Can you describe the man?" Derrick continued.

"He was big, white, about five-eleven, a little chunky and wore dark clothes. He had a hat pulled low over his eyes, and kept looking down. And it was dark, late last night when he pulled in. We get a lot of truckers in here, and I thought he was one of them."

"But he wasn't?" Derrick confirmed.

"Wasn't driving no big rig."

"What was he driving?"

She twisted the ends of her faded blouse. "I don't know cars, but it was one of them SUVs. Black."

"What about the license number?" Sheriff Cramer inquired.

"Didn't see it." She worked her mouth from side to side. "I'm sorry. I reckon I'm not being much help."

"No," Brianna ventured softly. "Anything you can tell us is helpful." The man she'd described could have been the one who'd broken into her house.

And at least the baby was alive.

"What time did he leave?" Derrick asked.

The woman worked her mouth again. "Around dawn. The truckers usually leave early. But he seemed especially in a hurry. He tore out of here like a bat out of hell."

"Did you see which way he was going?"

"Headed up the parkway going north."

"Was anyone else with him? A woman maybe?"

"Yeah, some blond bimbo. I didn't see her face though, just that brassy hair. I wouldn't have noticed her at all if they hadn't been arguing. She yelled at him, and he told her to shut up and get in the car."

"Is there anything else you can tell us?" the sheriff added.

The woman waddled around behind the counter, then reached for something and put it on the counter. "I found this little pair of booties on the floor of their room after they left."

Brianna picked them up, tears swelling in her eyes. "They're Ryan's," she said. "I bought them for him last week."

DERRICK HEARD THE DESPAIR IN Brianna's voice and wanted to reassure her that this information was a good sign, but he wasn't sure it was.

The couple the woman had described didn't match the Hamptons or the Phillipses. Worse, if the man and woman were arguing, they might have fought about the kidnapping, which meant the situation could get volatile.

Little Ryan might be affected. Even hurt.

And if one party wasn't into the game, that one might be tempted to dump the baby.

A baby abandoned in this kind of weather wouldn't survive twenty-four hours.

His throat convulsed at the thought. He didn't want to see another child's grave.

Especially his own son's.

He fisted his hands by his sides, a bead of perspiration trickling down his cheek. No, he'd find him and bring him home safely. He had to.

"What name did the man use to check in?" Sheriff Cramer asked.

The woman glanced down at the register. "John Smith."

Derrick grimaced. Of course, that was fake. "How did he pay?"

"Cash."

"Has the room been cleaned yet?" Derrick persisted.

"No. When I saw that Amber Alert, I held off."

Derrick offered a smile. "Good."

"I'll get a CSI team to search the room for prints and forensics," Cramer said.

Derrick placed his business card on the counter. "If you think of anything else, please call."

Cramer shot him a warning look as if he'd overstepped his bounds, but Derrick ignored him. Cramer phoned in the description of the man and SUV and asked his deputy to send the information out to the other authorities, then retrieved the room key, punched in another number for the crime lab and requested a unit to the motel.

Derrick and Brianna followed him to the room, but the sheriff insisted they stay outside so as not to contaminate evidence. But one glance inside and Derrick knew finding and sorting out forensics wouldn't be easy. Judging from the stained carpet, faded bedspread, musty odors and dust, this room had seen hundreds of visitors and very little pine cleaner or bleach.

"You need to let me handle this investigation," Cramer reiterated.

Derrick squared his shoulders. "I'm just trying to help."

"By accusing Dana Phillips of kidnapping?" Cramer scraped a hand over the side of his face. "She's threatening to press charges against you for harassment."

Brianna cleared her throat. "Beau, listen, I'm really sorry we upset her. But we didn't actually accuse her of anything. We just asked some questions."

"In a kidnapping, we have to explore every angle," Derrick said. "Sometimes we have to ask tough questions and people get pissed. But that's the only way to uncover the truth." He hesitated, trying to rein in his temper and his own desperation. "And this woman was angry that Brianna adopted Natalie's baby. Dana wanted Ryan herself."

"You should have come to me," Cramer complained. "I would have followed that lead."

"You were busy with the crime unit at Brianna's," Derrick countered through clenched teeth. "Besides, you held back important information yourself."

Cramer's expression darkened. "What the hell are you talking about?"

Derrick stood his ground. "That you dated Natalie."

Cramer's mouth thinned into a frown. "I didn't think it was relevant."

"Not relevant?" Derrick repeated. "I left my DNA with you for a paternity test, and you didn't bother to share that you might have fathered the baby." He pointed a finger at Cramer. "That gives you motive, Cramer, that's the reason you didn't confess the truth."

"There's nothing to confess." Cramer scowled. "We dated a few times a while back, no big deal."

"When was it?" Derrick pressed.

"I don't know exactly. Like I said, a few months ago."

Derrick wanted to slam his fist into the cop's nose. "Think, dammit. When? Could Ryan be yours?"

"No," Cramer said. "I confronted Natalie after she got pregnant, and she told me the baby wasn't mine. I even offered to marry her, but she turned me down."

"So you were in love with her?" Derrick suggested.

Cramer shrugged. "Yeah, but she didn't want marriage.

Not even with a baby. I can't imagine why a chick would want to go that route alone."

"When she rejected you, you were pissed?" Derrick asked.

Cramer stepped forward as if he might hit him. "Listen to me, McKinney. I did not kidnap that baby. And I'm doing everything I can to find him. So don't hold things back from me again."

IF BRIANNA HAD WONDERED HOW Derrick had felt about Natalie, she knew now. He and Beau Cramer had both been in love with her.

Why hadn't Natalie accepted Beau's proposal? Because Ryan was Derrick's son, and she'd been in love with him?

Brianna sighed. She certainly understood why. Derrick had a masculine presence that was irresistible. Watching him in action was even more impressive. His strength, intelligence and drive gave her confidence and hope.

Still, the kidnapper possessed a violent streak. What if Ryan cried and the man lost his temper?

"Will you keep me posted on what you learn from the search party and forensics?" Derrick asked.

Cramer gave a clipped nod. "And if you do uncover any other suspects, let me know. I don't need you running all over town accusing the locals of kidnapping."

Derrick glanced at Brianna, and she sighed. "I did discover that Rhoda Hampton had another miscarriage."

"Good grief, did you go accuse her, too?" the sheriff asked.

She shook her head. "We went to her duplex to talk to her, but she wasn't home."

"She and her husband both left town," Derrick said. "The timing is suspicious. You might look into that."

Cramer studied them as if he didn't know whether to trust them, but finally conceded with a nod.

Still, Brianna was grateful Derrick had his own men on the case.

Derrick slid a hand to Brianna's waist. "Come on, Brianna, he can handle it here. Let's grab something to eat and go home. You need rest."

Brianna wanted to argue, but her head was throbbing, and fatigue weighed her body down. She pulled her coat around her as they walked to the car, more snow flurries beginning to drift down from the gray clouds. Daylight was waning, the days shorter now with winter approaching, the dismal sky adding to her bleak mood.

What had the man and woman been arguing over? Something to do with the baby?

Her stomach spasmed at the thought of them harming him.

When she settled into the car, she rested her head against the seat and closed her eyes. The image of little Ryan wrapped in the hospital blanket flashed in her mind, along with other images from the past few weeks.

Ryan cuddling against her as she'd held him. His tiny feet and hands waving as he bicycled them in the crib. His big brown eyes staring at the teddy bear mobile above his bed, the way he'd watched it spin around while it played "Twinkle, Twinkle Little Star." The tiny noises he'd made, the gurgles and coos when she'd bathed him.

She must have dozed off because the next time she opened her eyes, they'd stopped at Delilah's Diner.

"Brianna, I know you're wiped out," Derrick stated. "But something you said at the school is bothering me."

She pushed a strand of hair off her forehead and opened her eyes. "What?"

"You asked if Natalie had been acting oddly the last few weeks. What did you mean by that?"

Brianna chewed her lip, debating on whether she'd read too much into Natalie's behavior.

"Bri, tell me."

"I don't know if I just imagined it, but the last few weeks before she died, Natalie acted...differently."

He gave her a sideways glance. "What do you mean?"

Brianna massaged her temple. "Secretive. Nervous. As if something was on her mind." She released a pent-up breath. "I thought she was simply anxious about the baby coming. But the night I drove her to the E.R. to have Ryan, she seemed almost panicked."

"Panicked? About childbirth?"

Brianna shrugged. "I thought so at first, but as the nurse wheeled her into the E.R., she made me swear that if anything happened to her, that I'd take care of the baby. I tried to assure her that nothing bad would happen, that everything would be all right. But she grabbed my hands and insisted." She paused, then decided to share her worst fear. "It was almost as if she knew she was going to die."

Derrick studied her for a long moment. "Did she mention anything specific that spooked her?"

A chill skated along her arms. "Yes. One night we had dinner and on the way home she seemed jumpy. She kept looking over her shoulder as if she was scared. As if she thought someone might be following her."

"And then she died," Derrick said.

"I know," Brianna whispered. "It just seemed—"

"Suspicious."

She gave a pained nod.

"And now someone has kidnapped her child." Derrick shifted on the balls of his feet. "You're right, that does sound suspicious. Maybe we need to look into Natalie's death and make sure she died of natural causes." He swung the vehicle toward the rental cabins on Raven's Ridge. "I'm going to pick up some things before we go to your house."

She jerked her head toward him. "That's not necessary."

"I'll sleep on your couch, but I'm not leaving you alone."

Brianna twined her fingers together, her heart pounding. Was it possible that Natalie had been murdered?

THE BABY WAILED FROM THE backseat as the man wound up Blue Ridge Parkway. "Can't you shut him up?"

His girlfriend rolled her eyes, but continued to file her fingernails. "I told you I wasn't no mother."

He jerked the nail file from her fingers. "Well, try," he snarled. "Or I'm going to dump you both."

She made a pouty face. "Then you'll have to find some place to stop. I can't reach his car seat from here."

"All right," he grumbled. "There's probably a truck stop up ahead."

He flipped on the radio to drown out the baby's cries.

"Regarding the Amber Alert for baby Ryan, the six-week-old kidnapped from his adoptive home this morning, the child is still missing. Authorities now believe that the man who stole the child may be traveling with a blond female. They were last seen driving toward the Blue Ridge Parkway in a dark SUV. If you spot this couple or their vehicle, please call the sheriff."

He slammed his fist against the steering wheel. Dammit.

"They know who we are," she screeched.

"They don't have our names," he growled. "But they will be looking for us, and we need to get rid of this vehicle."

He spotted a sign for a truck stop up ahead and veered onto the exit. He'd ditch the SUV, steal another car and then get back on the road.

And the sooner he dumped the kid, the better. Then he could put some distance between him and this mess, and no one could link the baby's disappearance to him.

Chapter Seven

A haunting silence hung in the house as Brianna and Derrick entered, the air filled with memories of what had happened that morning. Derrick flipped a light switch, and the Christmas tree lights twinkled merrily, but the small packages beneath the tree, the stocking she'd made for Ryan, and the fact that he might not be home for the holidays made her heart ache.

She wanted to dress him in the little red sleeper she'd bought and make a Christmas photo as Natalie would have done. Make cookies with him when he got older. String popcorn and buy him a puppy and see the magic in his eyes when Santa left surprises beneath the tree.

Derrick had picked up two specials at the diner for them, and took them to the kitchen. "Come and sit down, Brianna and eat."

"I'm really not hungry," she said.

He took her by the arm. "You haven't eaten anything all day. It won't help Ryan if you end up sick."

Her body was aching, but she was too tired to argue, so she slumped into the kitchen chair. The scent of

Delilah's beef stew wafted toward her, and she managed to eat at least half the food, while Derrick inhaled his.

"I've been thinking about what you said about Natalie being nervous, seeming afraid," Derrick told her. "Did you keep any of Natalie's things after she died?"

Brianna leaned her head on her hand. "A few things. I boxed them up and they're in the extra bedroom. Her computer is there, too." She hesitated. "I didn't know what to do with it."

"I'd like to look through them. Maybe I'll find some clues."

Like Ryan's father's name.

"Of course you can go through them," Brianna concurred.

"Go take a hot bath and lie down. You need some rest, Bri."

"How can I sleep when Ryan is out there somewhere, God knows where? What if this man hurts him, Derrick?"

Derrick rose, then cradled her elbow in his and coaxed her to stand. "You have to try. When we bring Ryan home, and we will, you need to have your energy back."

She nodded, although her mind screamed with self-recriminations. If only she'd woken up five minutes earlier. If she'd had Ryan in her room. If she'd been stronger…

"Come on." He urged her toward the stairs. "A hot bath will help your sore muscles. And I'll fix you some tea or a drink, whatever you want to help you sleep."

"Hot tea would be good," she said quietly. "That and some painkillers."

He walked her through her bedroom to the bath and bent to turn on the water. Slowly his dark gaze rose to meet hers. His eyes flickered with amber and gold flecks, and skated over her with such intensity that her body tingled. "Do you need help?"

A blush crept up her face. Had he read her mind? "No. I can manage." The idea of Derrick helping her undress would have sounded appealing under different circumstances, but she didn't want him to see her battered body now.

Especially after he'd been with Natalie. Natalie was beautiful and had the perfect body. Big breasts. Thin hips. Experience with men.

His eyes darkened again as if he wanted to touch her, but a second later, he averted his gaze and she assumed she'd imagined it. "Then I'll go make the tea and look into Natalie's things."

The mention of her deceased friend's belongings tossed water on the spark of desire that had rippled through her, and she nodded, then watched him leave the room.

He had been in love with Natalie. And he might be Ryan's father.

Nothing could ever happen between them.

DERRICK SILENTLY CURSED himself. For a minute when he'd looked at Brianna, he'd imagined undressing her and had itched to remove her clothes. To touch her and hold her and console her.

To kiss her and assuage her pain.

But reality quickly intruded. He had a job to do. To find Ryan. To know for sure what had happened with Natalie. If she could possibly have been murdered.

He couldn't let Brianna get under his skin.

Women were not to be trusted.

After all, she might have known Ryan was his son and kept it from him.

If she had, he couldn't forgive that.

Figuring it would take Brianna a while to bathe, he put on the water for the tea, then retrieved the box holding Natalie's things and her laptop. His gaze fell on Ryan's photos, and he walked over to study them.

Ryan was a plump little baby with dark blond hair and brown eyes. Hair and eyes like his.

Ryan had to be his son.

Maybe there was something in that box or on her computer to prove it. He lowered himself on the sofa and dug through the box. A few photographs of Natalie and Brianna when they were younger, a silk scarf, certificates of awards Natalie had received in high school, her college degree, three yearbooks from the high school.

Nothing to verify that he was the baby's father or indicate what had upset Natalie those last few months.

While he booted up her computer, he heard the tea-kettle whistle, so he made the tea, then carried it up the steps. He'd search Natalie's browser and e-mails once Brianna was asleep.

It was quiet as he approached Brianna's bedroom, and he knocked softly, but she didn't answer.

Concern caught in his chest. She'd been through hell today, both physically and emotionally, and should have been in bed instead of running all over town. But she'd toughed it out to find the baby.

His son.

Because she loved him, too.

He knocked again, but once more she didn't respond, so he tiptoed inside. The bathroom door was ajar, and he spotted her lying back in a sea of bubbles, her head on a bath pillow, her eyes closed.

He paused, his breath catching again, this time at the beautiful picture she painted. She'd swept her ebony hair up on top of her head. But soft tendrils had escaped and fallen around her cheeks. Cheeks pale and bruised from the kidnapper when she'd fought to save his son.

Bubbles covered most of her body, dotting the soft curve of her breasts, but one puckered nipple slipped through the cloud. The sight of it stirred his lust. And her lips were slightly parted as if she'd finally given into fatigue and fallen asleep.

He had always admired Brianna when they were young, had thought she possessed a quiet strength and spunk, especially knowing her past. And he'd secretly always wanted her.

But it was nothing compared to the hunger flaring inside him now.

She looked soft and sweet and vulnerable, and he wanted to kiss those pink lips.

Unable to resist, he placed the tea on the bath vanity, then walked over and brushed the hair from her cheek. Her eyes slowly fluttered open, filled with the haze of sleep and confusion.

A second later, they widened as if reality intruded, and she crossed her arms over her breasts. Instead of hiding her though, the movement sent water sloshing over the tub, revealing both voluptuous breasts. They were firm and high but swayed as she moved, her nipples stiffening as they met the cool air.

His body hardened, but the sight of the black and purple bruises on her torso made his jaw clench in fury.

"Dammit, you should have gone to the hospital."

Embarrassment heated her cheeks, and she lowered her gaze. "Hand me a towel, please."

He reached for the towel, and she grabbed it from him. "You can leave now."

He raked his gaze over her once more, wanting to help her up, but sensing he'd already said too much. So he turned and walked to the door.

But her soft moan of pain made him race back to her. She was doubled over, gripping her chest in an attempt to breathe through the pain and clinging to the wall with her other hand.

Ignoring the glare she gave him, he grabbed the towel and wrapped it around her, then lifted her from the tub.

"I'm fine," she grumbled through gritted teeth.

"The hell you are." He grabbed another towel and dried her feet and shoulders off, again ignoring her protests, then picked her up and carried her to her bed. He yanked the covers back, then gently eased her down on the sheets.

"Do you have an Ace bandage?" he asked.

She breathed in and out. "In the cabinet below the bathroom sink."

He hurried to retrieve it, then lowered himself on the bed beside her and reached for the towel.

"I can do it myself." She lifted her chin defiantly.

"Stop being so stubborn," he said in a low whisper.

With one quick flick, he lowered the towel then began to wrap her ribs.

She closed her eyes and clenched her jaw, and he forced himself not to kiss her bruises when he wanted to press his lips to her skin and ease her pain.

And make them both forget that Ryan was still missing and might never be found.

MORTIFICATION STAINED Brianna's cheeks, but she closed her eyes and allowed Derrick to tend to her. All day she'd fought not to break down in front of him and struggled not to give in to the pain racking her body, but it had taken its toll. Even the hot bath hadn't alleviated the throbbing in her chest and head.

"Where's your gown?" he asked in a voice so soothing and full of understanding that tears blurred her eyes. No one had ever taken such tender care of her without asking something in return.

She pushed aside the bad childhood memories and focused on the present. She'd long since let go of the past.

Of her mother and the boyfriends who'd passed through their house, virtually strangers in the night. Strangers who sometimes liked little girls....

The reason her mother had finally dropped her at the orphanage. To protect her, she'd said.

But Brianna had known the real reason—her mother had chosen the men over her.

She'd vowed never to follow in her footsteps. Never to *need* a man. Never to put him before her child.

But in doing so she'd shut down, hadn't developed a relationship because she was all closed up inside.

Because she didn't trust. And without trust she couldn't love or be loved.

Don't be silly. Derrick loved Natalie, not you. You're just a tool to find his son.

"Brianna?"

"In the top dresser drawer."

She forced her eyes open, to gather her pride as he dug through her drawer and returned with a flannel nightshirt. He helped her ease it on, then pulled the covers over her.

"The tea might be cold by now."

"It's fine," she said. "I think I just need to close my eyes for a minute."

He patted her arm. "Get some rest, Brianna."

"Did you find anything in Natalie's things?" she asked.

"Not yet, but I'm going to search her computer now." He flipped off the light. "Call me if you need me. I'll be downstairs."

She sighed and nestled in the covers, then closed her eyes. Maybe she could sleep for a few minutes, then she'd get up and help him. Hopefully by that time, he'd have some answers, and they would know where to look for Ryan.

And when they did…

For a moment, she allowed herself to fantasize that they would bring him home together, that the two of them would raise him as theirs.

But reality nagged at her, and she knew that the DNA test would prove that Ryan belonged to Derrick. He'd already said that when they brought him home, he would fight for custody.

And he would win, move on and leave her behind.

DERRICK FORCED HIMSELF TO leave Brianna's room when he really wanted to crawl in bed beside her, pull her into his arms and hold her. She looked so damn vulnerable and soft, but so damn strong, that his lungs constricted, and for a moment, he simply watched her sleep. For the life of him, even though he wanted to mistrust her and steel himself against caring about her, he was having a hard time doing so.

But Ryan was missing. And he had to save him and give him the future the innocent little boy deserved.

Grateful she was finally resting, he jogged down the steps then focused on Natalie's computer, skimming her e-mails for anything suspicious. Several work-related messages filled a file, along with a few personal notes from friends and acquaintances. But nothing that stirred his suspicions. Not even another boyfriend or lover.

He logged onto the Internet and found a MySpace page and skimmed her interests, her song choices and friends, but again found nothing that indicated problems or that anyone had a grudge against Natalie.

Then he found a reference to a personal journal, so he clicked on the icon for the pages and began to read the entries. First, she talked about her and Brianna and their close friendship, about how Brianna had always told her that she'd saved her years ago when she'd befriended her, but Natalie had looked up to Brianna instead.

Next, he read several entries about her job and her internal debate over whether to leave town. Then a reference to trouble with a few students. One in particular she thought might be involved with drugs. A reference to a conversation where the boy had become belligerent.

Then a different reference to a teen at Magnolia Manor she suspected might be involved in drugs.

He made a note of the names to check them out.

He skimmed a few more entries, then sat up, taking notice at a mention of him.

> I was really nervous and uptight about everything going on at the school. And I took a trip to Raleigh and ran into Derrick McKinney. God, I made a big mistake. I had too much to drink and hooked up with him, and now I don't know how to tell Bri. I know she's had a crush on him for years, and she'll hate me if she finds out.

Perspiration trickled down his forehead. Bri had a crush on him?

Why had she never said anything? Never let him know?

Then the realization of Natalie's note set in. Bri knew he and Natalie had been together so eventually Natalie told her about that night. If she'd been standoffish before, had not shown her feelings, she sure as hell wouldn't now.

Especially when he and Natalie might have shared a son. A son Natalie had asked Bri to raise, and never told him about.

Why hadn't Natalie wanted him in her baby's life? Because she didn't think he was father material?

Battling the pain that thought triggered, he scrolled through a few more pages until he discovered another entry that made him pause.

Today I heard some of the kids talking about The Club. They said it had started up again, just like eight years ago. They were whispering about something awful that had happened back then, some kind of explosion that had killed dozens of people.

I went to Principal Billings and asked him about it, but he told me that he would check into it, that I shouldn't ask questions, that it would be dangerous if I did.

Tonight, someone tried to run me off the road and I almost crashed. I don't know what to do or whom to trust.

I want to tell Bri, but what if confiding in her puts her in danger, too?

Derrick balled his hands into fists. Tomorrow he would talk to Principal Billings about this club. He'd also visit the hospital and inquire about Natalie's death.

If he didn't get the answers he wanted, he'd talk to Beau Cramer and arrange to have Natalie's body exhumed.

An autopsy would tell them if she had been murdered.

Chapter Eight

By dawn the next morning, Derrick had showered, dressed and had coffee ready. He also checked in with Ben and Running Deer, but there were no new developments. He was drinking his third cup when he heard Brianna rambling around upstairs.

She looked more rested when she came down the steps, although her eyes remained haunted, the bruise on her cheek still stark.

"Did you sleep?" he asked.

She didn't look at him, but nodded and poured herself a cup of coffee. "Did you?"

"I'm fine," Derrick said. "I looked through Natalie's computer last night and discovered a personal journal."

Brianna claimed the chair facing him at the table. "Did it help?"

"Maybe." He cradled the mug between his hands to keep from touching her cheek, from asking her if she was still in pain, from kissing the tender skin and pulling her to him. Her slow movements indicated she was hurting, but she'd latched on to the stubborn determination he'd seen the day before and wouldn't complain.

"What?" Brianna asked, jerking his mind back on track.

He bypassed the personal entries about him, and the fact that Natalie said Bri had had a crush on him. Had she really?

"In her journal, Natalie noted that there might be a meth lab somewhere, that she'd heard some teens talking about it."

"A meth lab?"

"Yes. She also mentioned a club and something that had happened eight years ago. She talked to the principal about it, but he told her that he'd check into it, and warned her it was too dangerous for her to ask questions."

"What kind of club?"

"I don't know, but I intend to find out." He sipped his coffee. "But you were right. Natalie was scared. Someone tried to run her off the road. She wanted to tell you, but she was afraid confiding would endanger you."

Brianna's troubled gaze met his. "She tried to protect me."

He nodded. "But she was scared, and if she stumbled onto something that this club wanted kept quiet, maybe they caused her death."

"The doctor *was* vague," Brianna recounted. "But why kidnap Ryan?"

"I don't know, unless they were afraid that Natalie told you something."

A look of dawning stretched across Brianna's face as if she'd suddenly remembered something. "I did go back to the hospital and ask questions about her death," she said.

Derrick stood. "We need to talk to the principal and that doctor again."

Brianna glanced at the phone. "It's been over twenty-four hours, Derrick. Why won't they call?"

Derrick gritted his teeth so hard his jaw ached. The only explanation he could think of was that this wasn't a kidnapping for ransom.

And if they didn't want money, they didn't intend to return the baby.

NATALIE'S COMMENTS IN HER journal worried Brianna. She'd sensed her friend had been frightened, but having her suspicions confirmed added a different spin to Ryan's kidnapping.

"Why don't we divide up when we go inside?" Derrick suggested as they parked in front of the high school. "I'll meet with the principal while you talk to some of the teachers."

Brianna nodded. Thankfully, she'd visited the school for her job before so being seen in the hallways wouldn't raise a red flag. They entered the building, and Derrick went straight to the principal's office. She walked down the hall to the teacher's lounge first, hoping to find a couple of teachers there for coffee or during their free period, and she lucked out.

Pauline Brown, an English teacher, and Seth Ingram who taught Health, were getting coffee and doughnuts.

"Oh, my gosh, Brianna, what happened to your face?" Pauline asked.

"Have you found the baby?" Seth inquired.

Brianna had attempted to hide the worst with makeup, but her efforts obviously failed. "I fought with the kidnapper," Brianna said. "And no, we haven't found Ryan. That's why I'm here."

"I don't understand." Pauline folded her hands. "How can we help?"

"In Natalie's journal, she admitted she was afraid. She also mentioned something about a meth lab and a club. That something bad that happened eight years ago. Do you know anything about this club or the meth lab?"

Pauline frowned. "No, but I wouldn't be surprised that the kids knew about a meth lab. The mountains are probably full of them."

Seth grimaced. "Unfortunately she's right. But what does this have to do with Natalie? I thought she died in childbirth."

The door opened and Evan Rutherford, the high school football coach, loped in.

"I don't know yet," Brianna claimed. "But someone tried to run Natalie off the road. Then she went into labor the next week and died. And now her baby Ryan has been kidnapped."

"All of that does seem strange," Pauline commented.

"So what are you saying?" Seth asked. "That Natalie didn't die in childbirth?"

Brianna shrugged. "I'm not sure. I'm just trying to find out what happened to her and why someone would take Ryan." She glanced at Evan but he poured himself a cup of coffee and remained silent.

Brianna folded her arms. "What about this club? Have you heard of it?"

Pauline pinched the edge of a cinnamon doughnut. "No."

"Me neither," Seth said.

Brianna twisted her hands together. "If you all think or hear of anything that could help, please call me." She ducked out the door and headed down the hall to Sarah Keefer's room. Sarah and Natalie had taught side-by-side for two years now. If Natalie had confided her fears to anyone here, it was probably to Sarah.

The bell to change classes rang just as she arrived at Sarah's room, and she stepped aside as teenagers poured from the room and flooded the halls. Sarah spotted her and rushed toward her.

"Good heavens, Brianna. You look horrible." She gave her a hug. "I'm so sorry about Ryan. Have you heard any news?"

She shook her head. "No, and I have to ask you something. And I need the truth."

Sarah's lips grew pinched. "The truth about what?"

Brianna explained about Natalie's journal. "Did she tell you what she was afraid of or mention this club?"

Sarah fidgeted. "You really think this might have something to do with Ryan being kidnapped?"

"It's possible, Sarah." She clutched her hand. "Please, tell me what you know."

Sarah lowered her voice. "Natalie said that she'd heard about a meth lab and discussed it with Principal Billings. He told her that he'd look into it, that it was dangerous for her, but as she was leaving, she over-heard him make a phone call."

"What exactly did she overhear?"

"Principal Billings mentioned The Club, and that he was worried about what happened eight years ago, that they couldn't let the truth get out." Sarah tucked a strand of her curly hair behind her ear. "Later Natalie admitted that she was really scared, and that she was thinking of leaving town once the baby was born."

Brianna grimaced. Apparently Principal Billings was hiding something.

And if it had anything to do with Natalie's death or Ryan being missing, she'd see that he paid.

DERRICK'S PHONE BUZZED WHILE he waited to see the principal, and he checked the caller ID box.

Larry Hampton.

Hoping the man had news, he quickly connected the call. "Derrick McKinney speaking."

"Mr. McKinney, this is Larry Hampton. You left a message for me to call you."

"Yes. I'm working with Guardian Angel Investigations, and we're investigating the kidnapping of Ryan Cummings Honeycutt."

A tense silence vibrated over the line, then a labored sigh. "What does that have to do with me?"

Derrick would have preferred to meet with the man in person, but a phone interview would have to suffice. "I don't know if it does or not, but I'm investigating all possibilities."

"Why call me?" Hampton asked. "I don't even know the Honeycutt woman."

"I understand that your wife recently lost a baby, Mr. Hampton."

"Who told you that?"

"It doesn't matter. And I am sorry for your loss. But I also understand that an emotional trauma like she suffered could have caused her to do something rash... something she normally wouldn't do."

"You're accusing my wife of kidnapping that baby?" Anger radiated strong and clear in the man's voice. "I can't believe this crap."

"Look, Mr. Hampton. I'm not accusing her of anything. But I have to explore every option, and it would help if I spoke with her. If for no other reason than to eliminate her as a suspect."

Hampton cursed. "Talking to her is not an option."

"Protecting her won't do you any good."

"I have to protect her, she's my wife," Hampton said. "But it's not what you think. Rhoda didn't kidnap that baby."

"Then let me talk to her myself."

"I said no."

"Why not? It's either me or the sheriff."

Another low curse. "You can't talk to her because she's been admitted to the hospital in the psychiatric ward." His voice broke. "My wife tried to commit suicide, Mr. McKinney. I carried her to the E.R. myself two days ago."

The day before Ryan went missing. Damn.

"I'm sorry," Derrick said and meant it. "I hope she gets help, Mr. Hampton."

Hampton released a weary sigh. "I hope you find the baby, too."

The line went silent, and Derrick snapped his phone shut, then looked up to see Brianna standing beside him. "Who was that?"

He relayed details from Hampton's call.

"I'm sorry to hear about her suicide attempt," Brianna said in a strained voice. "Have you talked to Principal Billings?"

"Not yet, I've been waiting."

"We need to push him for answers." She passed on what Sarah had revealed, and he grimaced.

Principal Billings opened his door and gestured for them to come in. Derrick introduced himself, and Brianna shook his hand, then Derrick explained the reason for their visit.

"We know Natalie talked to you about a meth lab," Derrick confirmed. "And that you said that you'd look into it, that it was too dangerous for her. What did you mean by that?"

Principal Billings claimed his desk chair, picked up a pen and began to roll it between his fingers. "Sometimes kids involved in drugs can be dangerous."

"Why specifically for her?"

Billings looked rattled. "I meant it would be dangerous for anyone."

"Did these kids belong to some kind of club?" Brianna cut in.

Shock widened his eyes for a moment before he

masked it. "I don't know. I have teachers listening out to see if we can narrow down any specific students who might be involved in drugs."

"Natalie was afraid after she talked to you," Brianna said. "She mentioned leaving town after her baby was born. We're wondering if someone from this club thought she knew too much and wanted to keep her quiet."

Billings rolled his pen between his fingers more frantically. "Like I said, I asked her to let me take care of things. If there is a meth lab and my kids are involved, I'll put a stop to it."

"What do you know about the club and how it's related to something that happened eight years ago?" Derrick asked.

Billings dropped the pen, then tugged at the collar of his shirt. "Nothing."

Derrick crossed his arms, his voice hard. "Natalie overheard you on the phone, Mr. Billings. What happened eight years ago that has you afraid?"

"I don't know what you're talking about." He stood, glanced at his calendar then gestured toward the door. "I really don't understand what this has to do with the baby kidnapping, but I hope you find the child. Now, please excuse me. I have another appointment."

Derrick stood but held his ground. "If you're hiding something, Billings, we'll find out and be back. And if you know anything that could help us locate Ryan, you'd better speak up. If not, you can be held as a conspirator in a kidnapping case. And—"

He made a point of looking around the office. "If we discover Natalie didn't die of natural causes, an accomplice to murder."

BRIANNA FOLLOWED DERRICK OUT to the car, her nerves on edge as the hours and minutes ticked by.

Hours and minutes that meant Ryan was getting farther and farther away from her. Hours and minutes that meant that they might never bring him home.

"I know Principal Billings is not telling us everything," she declared as they fastened their seat belts. "But what if we're wasting time on a wild goose chase? What if this lab has nothing to do with the kidnapping?"

Derrick sighed, ran his hand through his hair, and glanced at her, his eyes full of turmoil. Her heart squeezed for him. He'd been strong, taking care of her, and pursuing every lead.

But this investigation had to be tearing him apart inside. He'd loved Natalie as she had, and his son was missing.

Yes, she knew Ryan was Derrick's. When she'd first seen Derrick at her house when she'd regained consciousness, she'd noticed the similarities. His strong nose and jaw. His dark blond hair and deep brown eyes.

Eyes that sucked a girl in.

"Brianna," Derrick began, "I've worked a lot of cases. The Amber Alert is out with Ryan's photo. And we have to follow every lead we have."

"But—"

"Shh." He took her hand and pulled it into his. The warm contact soothed her nerves slightly and she clung to his voice.

"Most kidnappings are personally related, meaning

that the kidnapper knows the victim. Since neither you nor Natalie had money, we have to believe that."

She nodded, needing to trust him, to cling to hope. "Where are we going now?"

"The hospital."

They lapsed into silence, and she felt the tension coiling inside him as they entered the hospital.

Dr. Thorpe, the doctor who delivered Ryan was in surgery, so they were forced to wait. Derrick insisted they have lunch, and she managed to swallow a few bites of a salad, but the food churned in her stomach.

An hour later, they met the doctor in his office. He looked at her with furrowed brows. "Miss Honeycutt, I didn't expect to see you again."

Derrick cleared his throat, then spoke in a take-charge voice and detailed their suspicions about Natalie's fears being related to Ryan's kidnapping.

"I don't understand," Dr. Thorpe said. "Natalie died of heart failure after the C-section."

Derrick frowned. "Is there any possible way someone could have slipped into the recovery room and injected Natalie with a drug that could have caused her death?"

"We have security," Dr. Thorpe noted. "And the staff here is well trained."

"Is it possible?" Derrick asked. "Most women who die in childbirth die of hemorrhaging. How many females in their twenties die of cardiac arrest?"

"A small percentage," Dr. Thorpe admitted.

"Too small and too coincidental considering the circumstances and things we've learned."

Silence stretched between them fraught with tension.

Dr. Thorpe pulled at his chin. "I suppose it's possible someone could have slipped in unnoticed on a busy night. But I don't really think that's what happened...."

In spite of his protests, doubts clouded the doctor's eyes.

Derrick lowered his voice to a lethal tone. "We're going to get to the bottom of all this, Dr. Thorpe. And the hospital had better be ready if we discover that you or anyone assisting you in any way caused Natalie's death."

DERRICK REMOVED HIS CELL PHONE from the inside of his jacket as they rode the elevator to the parking deck. He punched in Sheriff Cramer's number and shared what he'd learned so far.

"I told you to let me handle this investigation," Cramer repeated.

"Look, I'm calling you for help," Derrick snapped. "We don't have time to argue. If you really cared about Natalie, you'll get a warrant to have her body exhumed. It's imperative we know if there was foul play."

"I don't know if we have enough to convince a judge," Cramer said.

"Dammit, Cramer. You grew up around here. Use any pull you have."

Cramer hissed a deep breath. "All right. I'll see what I can do."

They reached the car, but Brianna paused and pointed to a note on his windshield. Derrick cursed as he read it.

Stop asking questions or you'll never see the baby again.

Brianna paled as she read it over his shoulder, and reached for the car door. But his instincts kicked in, and he grabbed her arm and held her back. "Wait."

Years of experience warned him to check beneath the car. He squatted down and looked underneath the vehicle, and his breath stopped.

A bomb was strapped below the engine, then a clicking sounded, and he realized someone had triggered it.

"There's a bomb! Run!" He grabbed Brianna, and raced toward the grassy area beside the parking lot.

The bomb exploded, metal flew, glass shattered and the impact tossed them to the ground.

Chapter Nine

Derrick covered Brianna with his body, taking the brunt of the metal and glass spewing through the air and pelting the asphalt. A second later, the gas tank exploded. The horrific sound jarred the air with smoke and the acrid scent of gas and burning rubble.

Brianna's body trembled beneath him, and he stroked her back to calm her.

"Are you okay, Bri?"

"Yes," she said hoarsely. "Are you?"

"Yeah." But if she hadn't noticed the note and he hadn't herded her away in time, they would both be dead. The realization sent fury rolling through him.

The sound of feet running and voices shouting drifted through the haze. He pivoted to see flames from the Jeep shooting upward, smoke billowing in the air. Heat radiated from the burning vehicle and thickened the air, suffocating in its intensity.

A man in a suit approached, two women beside him. "I called the paramedics."

"Good heavens, are you two all right?" one of the women asked.

Derrick shifted to his knees, then helped Brianna stand, and faced the spectators. "Yeah. Thanks."

"Was that a bomb?" the other woman asked.

Derrick clenched his jaw. "Yes, it was a bomb. I'm calling the sheriff now."

Questions pummeled him. Cramer had wanted to marry Natalie, and knew that Derrick had slept with her. Could he trust Cramer?

He had no choice, though. He had to report this. And surely Cramer wouldn't do something so stupid as to set off a bomb in front of a hospital.

Two paramedics jogged toward them, but he waved them off from examining him, and they turned to Brianna to make sure she wasn't hurt. Two security guards from the hospital appeared and began to corral the crowd to keep spectators from getting too close. He removed his phone and quickly punched in Cramer's direct number.

"Sheriff Cramer."

"It's Derrick McKinney. Someone just tried to kill me and Brianna."

Cramer cursed. "What happened?"

The fire engine raced up, siren wailing and screeched to a stop. Derrick covered the phone so he could hear over the noise as the firefighters jumped into motion to extinguish the blazing vehicle.

"We stopped at the hospital to talk to the doctor who delivered Natalie's baby, and while we were inside, someone put a bomb under my SUV."

"Dammit, McKinney, I'll be right there. But I told you to let me ask the questions."

Derrick angled himself away from Brianna so she couldn't overhear his conversation.

"Cramer, I can't just sit on my ass. You know every hour a child is missing exponentially decreases the chance of finding the child alive. And Ryan has been missing for over twenty-four hours now."

"I'll send the CSI team over to search for clues. Why in the hell were you asking questions about Natalie's death?"

"I'll fill you in when you arrive. I want to check on Brianna." But first he phoned Ben and told him about the bomb. "Anything on the couple we discussed?"

"No. There's nothing suspicious about their finances, although the wife was seeing a therapist. But no property or other family."

Derrick sighed. "Do me a favor and check out Beau Cramer."

"The sheriff?"

"Yeah. He was in love with Natalie."

"I'll get right on it."

Derrick hung up and turned to see her staring at his SUV as the firefighters extinguished the blaze. She looked pale and bruised and frightened.

Anger churned through him at whomever had done this. He'd find the son of a bitch and make him sorry he ever touched Brianna or his son.

BRIANNA STARED AT THE BURNING SUV in shock. Metal and glass lay shattered on the asphalt and grass, embers of burning rubble lighting the ground like fireflies. The acrid scent of smoke and ashes thickened the air and created a blurry haze of gray against the sky.

Her stomach clenched. The past two days had been a virtual nightmare, and it seemed to be getting worse.

Ryan was still missing, they had no idea who had taken him, and the kidnapper was watching them—how else would he know that they'd been asking questions?

How else would he have known where she and Derrick were to plant that note and the bomb?

Other spectators had gathered to watch the firefighters hose down the vehicle, but she'd managed to convince the paramedics that she was unharmed so they'd retreated back inside the hospital.

Derrick approached her, the intense look in his eyes searing her. She folded her arms in an attempt to hold her emotions at bay, but Derrick's gaze met hers, and she felt herself crumbling.

"Bri…" Giving her a dark look, he pulled her into his arms.

She shuddered against him. "I can't believe this is happening," she whispered. "Why leave us a warning note when the kidnapper hasn't contacted us before? When he hasn't asked for money?"

He stroked her back in a comforting gesture and mumbled a soothing sound. She clutched his arms, burrowing against his warmth. "Because our asking questions is making him nervous."

Inhaling deeply to battle an onset of tears, she contemplated his answer then looked up into his eyes. "Then he thinks we're onto something?"

He shrugged. "Maybe. Why else would he warn us to stop asking questions?"

Brianna scanned the parking lot, the handful of spectators who'd gathered to watch the scene, wondering if the man was here now.

"But if he's watching us, where is Ryan?" The worst-case scenario flashed in her mind causing panic to claw at her chest.

Derrick's jaw tightened. "The motel clerk said the kidnapper was with a woman. He probably left the baby with her. Either that, or he's working with someone else."

The sheriff's car raced into the parking lot, siren wailing, and Derrick pulled away from her. "That's Cramer. I'll tell him what we found so far. Are you all right?"

She nodded, struggling for courage. How could she be all right knowing some maniac had tried to kill her? That he had Ryan?

That she might never see the little boy again?

DERRICK BRACED HIMSELF FOR another turf war over the investigation, but Cramer took one look at the charred piece of metal that used to be his SUV and hissed a breath. The deputy with him whistled as he spotted the scene, and Cramer ordered him to start stringing up crime scene tape to cordon off the area.

"Damn. This guy meant business," Cramer muttered as he approached.

Derrick nodded. "We need CSI to find out what kind of bomb it was. Maybe we'll luck out and get a print on one of the parts." Too damn bad the note had been destroyed in the explosion.

"I'll take care of it," Cramer said. He glanced at Brianna. "Are you all right?"

She nodded. "Yes, thanks to Derrick."

Her gaze met his, and a seed of emotion sprouted in his chest. Emotions he didn't want to feel for any woman, especially Brianna.

He still doubted if he would be a good father, but if Ryan was his son, he intended to fight for custody. That would mean going up against Brianna. And it was obvious she was already attached to the baby.

Cramer jerked his head to the messy scene. The last embers of the fire were dying, but the acrid smell of the burnt metal and smoke hung heavy in the air.

"What do you think precipitated this?" Cramer asked. "And what's this about wanting Natalie's body exhumed?"

Derrick glanced at Bri, then swallowed. "We have reason to suspect that Natalie might not have died of natural causes."

"What makes you suspect foul play?"

"Natalie was acting strangely the night I drove her to the E.R.," Brianna admitted. "I talked to some of the teachers at the high school where she taught, and two of them confirmed that she had been nervous."

"About what?" Cramer inquired.

"Apparently Natalie heard about a meth lab the teens might be involved in. When she reported it to the principal, he warned her it was too dangerous for her to look into, but that he would," Derrick said.

Brianna cleared her throat. "When we talked to him,

he said he was investigating, but he seemed nervous, too. And apparently Natalie admitted to one of her friends that she was scared, that she was thinking of leaving town once her baby was born."

Cramer shifted, removed a small notepad from his pocket, flipped it open and jotted something inside. "I don't understand. What was she afraid of?"

"I'm not sure," Brianna admitted. "But it had something to do with that meth lab and a club that had supposedly cropped up again."

"One that was involved with some kind of explosion that happened eight years ago," Derrick added.

Cramer frowned. "Eight years ago?"

"Yeah, I had left town for college by then. Do you remember what happened?"

Cramer glanced at the hospital. "There was an explosion at this very hospital back then. Dozens of people died, but the authorities never confirmed what happened or who created the mess."

"Oh, I do remember that," Brianna said.

"I was a senior at the time," Cramer reflected. "I lost my grandmother in it. It was the worst thing that has ever happened in Sanctuary. It nearly tore the town apart."

"Charlie's dad, Billy Driscill, was sheriff back then, wasn't he?" Derrick asked.

Cramer nodded. "He took a lot of heat for not solving the case. Finally ruled it accidental, but no one was satisfied with that answer."

Derrick glanced at Brianna. "We need to talk to Billy Driscill."

"I don't understand what this has to do with Natalie's death or Ryan being kidnapped," Brianna commented.

"Neither do I." Derrick frowned. "But if Natalie found out who was responsible for the explosion, and that person is still in town, he sure as hell wouldn't want the truth to be revealed."

"He might even kill to keep it quiet," Cramer guessed.

Brianna's face paled, and Derrick reached out to steady her. Natalie might have stumbled onto a secret no one wanted told. And if this club was responsible, there was most likely more than one person who wanted to keep the truth hidden.

"We need to get Natalie's body exhumed and do an autopsy," Derrick reiterated.

A muscle ticked in Cramer's jaw but he nodded. If the man had cared for Natalie, then he would want the truth, too. So finally they would be working on the same side.

Meanwhile he'd talk to Gage, see if he knew anything about the explosion that night or about this club.

If they could locate the club members, they might find the person who'd tried to run Natalie off the road.

And possibly the person who'd attacked Brianna, kidnapped Ryan and tried to kill them.

BRIANNA'S CHEST ACHED. BEAU was going to get a subpoena and have Natalie's body exhumed. She hated to think that her friend's grave would be disturbed, but if she had been murdered they needed to know.

Natalie deserved justice.

And why hadn't the doctor ordered an autopsy before? That question had nagged at her ever since the funeral. But she'd been too grief stricken immediately following Natalie's death—too preoccupied with making sure she got custody of Ryan and afraid someone would discover that she'd fudged papers—that she hadn't thought to push for one. She'd simply accepted the doctor's diagnosis.

Derrick gave her a concerned look, then spoke quietly to Beau and walked toward her. "Cramer's deputy is canvassing the crowd to see if someone saw or heard anything suspicious. I called a cab and I'll take you home."

Home, back to that empty silent house, to the crib that no longer held Ryan, to the Christmas tree that reminded her of his stocking and the presents she'd bought. Presents he might never receive. "What about your SUV?" she asked.

"I've got insurance."

She nodded and they walked up to the front of the hospital and met the cab.

"What do we do now?" she asked as the driver pulled from the parking lot.

"I'm going to call Gage and see what he knows about the explosion eight years ago. If this is connected, he might know who we should talk to."

She rested her head against the seat and closed her eyes. She was three years younger than Derrick, and remembered that year. She'd been living at Magnolia Manor with the others who'd never been adopted.

A faint memory stirred. "I should have thought about that explosion before," she said quietly. "But I didn't see a connection."

"What exactly do you recall?" Derrick asked.

She opened her eyes and frowned. "A lot of lost loved ones. A terrible sadness swept over Sanctuary. The mayor ordered the flag to be lowered to half mast, and then I heard gossip that the devil had come to town."

Derrick grunted. "The devil?"

"People were looking for someone to blame," she stated.

"What else do you remember?"

Her throat thickened. "One of the social workers who worked with Magnolia Manor coordinated adoptions for children placed at the Manor whose parents had died in the fire."

"Why does that stand out?"

"When I wasn't placed, she befriended me. She was the one who inspired me to pursue a similar career and work with adoptions."

Derrick cut her a dark look, then reached out and squeezed her hand. "That must have been tough for you."

"Yes, losing her was."

"I meant not being adopted."

Her old feelings of insecurities resurfaced. The feeling of abandonment. The sense that her mother hadn't loved her enough to keep her, or to come back for her.

The nagging question that something must be wrong with her—why else would her own parents not want her?

"I survived," she said, battling the emotions churning in her gut. She'd thought she'd put those feelings behind her.

And she had. Hadn't she?

Ryan's face flashed into her mind, and she bit her lip to keep from crying. They had to find Ryan. She couldn't let him grow up thinking that she and Natalie and his father had abandoned him.

Chapter Ten

Derrick contemplated how to move forward with the investigation during the drive back to Brianna's. The kidnapper had left a note on the car. Did that mean he intended to call with further instructions? That he planned to give Ryan back?

That he didn't want money but for them to leave the investigation alone?

Hadn't he known the kidnapping would raise questions?

Or maybe he'd planned to steal the baby, then kill Brianna and make her death look accidental or like natural causes as he had Natalie's?

"I'm going to shower," Brianna announced as they stepped inside her house. "I want to get rid of the stench of the smoke."

Knowing they might have died earlier twisted his insides. He wanted to join her. Hold her. Assure her that he would protect her and find Ryan. Soothe her bruises. Kiss away her fear.

Take her to bed and remind himself that they were both alive.

Hell, he'd been shot before, had nearly lost his life a half dozen times. But Brianna was an innocent. And she looked shell-shocked.

But Ryan was missing, and he couldn't afford to indulge his need for comfort—or his hunger for Brianna. Their probing into Natalie's past had obviously hit a nerve with the kidnapper, and he had to discover the reason.

So he watched her climb the stairs alone.

Even if teens had started up a meth lab, would they kill Natalie and kidnap a baby to cover it up?

That idea seemed far-fetched.

Or had Natalie uncovered something about that hospital explosion? Something that might lead them to know who had caused it and destroyed all those lives?

He hated to disturb Gage on his second honeymoon, but Gage might have known about this club.

He punched in the number of Gage's cell phone and studied baby Ryan's photos on the table while he waited. The little boy's chubby cheeks were rosy, his chin slightly square, his blond baby curls sending a pain through his chest.

Ryan had his square chin. His hair, although his own had darkened over the years, but as a baby it had been lighter than Ryan's. Emotions threatened to overcome him, and moisture dampened his eyes.

He hadn't cried in years. Not since the first of his father's beatings. Hell, he'd grown immune to those and had refused to give his father the pleasure of showing any weakness.

But fear for his baby threatened to bring him to his knees.

"Where are you, son?" he whispered.

Suddenly the call went through. "Gage McDermont."

"It's Derrick. I'm sorry to bother you on vacation."

"Don't worry about it, man. I talked to Ben about the kidnapping. How's the case going? Has Brianna received a ransom note or call?"

"No, not exactly." Derrick quickly brought him up to speed on the investigation, including the recent note and car explosion, their suspicions about Natalie's death possibly being a homicide, the questions they'd asked the doctor and what they'd learned at the school, then admitted his involvement with Natalie and his suspicions that Ryan was his son.

"God, Derrick, that must be hard as hell. Do you need me to come back and help you?"

"No. The team is good and I'm working with Cramer." Derrick hesitated. "What do you think of him?"

"So far, I haven't seen any problems. He seems bright, serious about this job. Why?"

Derrick sighed. "He was in love with Natalie."

"I see. Well, just watch your back."

"I will. Natalie seemed to think this lab might be related to the hospital explosion eight years ago. What do you know about that?"

A tense heartbeat of silence passed then Gage cleared his throat. "That was a bad night for a lot of reasons. A bunch of kids had a party and were passing around drugs."

"What kind of drugs?"

"A date rape drug for one. And I do remember my adopted brother Jerry talking about meth. But he and I weren't on good terms and I wanted nothing to do with it, so I didn't ask. I'd tell you to talk to him but Jerry left town last year after Ruby's kidnapping."

"Who else might know? I need to find out who belonged to this club," Derrick said. "If Natalie stumbled onto a lead into that hospital fire and the person who'd caused all those deaths is still in town, they might kill her to keep the truth from being revealed."

"You're right." Gage muttered a low sound of frustration. "Talk to Charlie Driscill and Evan Rutherford. They were at the party and might know."

Derrick gritted his teeth. "Charlie? He was acting sheriff after his dad retired and when Ruby was kidnapped last year, wasn't he?"

"Yeah, and he knew about the date rape drug. He helped me find Ruby, but then resigned, I think out of guilt." Gage released a labored sigh. "I'm not sure how cooperative he'll be, but since his father was sheriff back then, that would be the place to start."

BRIANNA COULDN'T SHAKE THE images of the explosion from her mind as she showered and dressed. She tried to cover the bruises with powder, but her eyes looked haunted, her face gaunt. She threw down the makeup. She didn't care what she looked like. All that mattered was finding the baby.

Had the person who'd set that bomb been standing by to watch? If he knew they'd survived, would he return to finish the job?

Had he hurt Ryan?

Her ribs were still sore, but she ignored the pain as she

descended the steps. Derrick had apparently rummaged through her refrigerator and cupboards and made some sandwiches. He glanced up at her with a tight smile.

"Do you feel better?"

"I'm okay."

He strode toward her, and rubbed her arms. "You keep saying that, but you don't look okay, Bri."

"How can I be?" she whispered. "If that man would kill us so coldly, what has he done to Ryan?"

Her voice cracked, and he pulled her to him and wrapped his arms around her. "I don't know, but that note makes me think he's alive."

His husky voice soothed her slightly, and she felt safe in his arms. Safe and cared for and tingly with the need to be closer to him. To have him kiss her and make her forget the horror that had become her life.

But Derrick was only being kind to her. He had loved Natalie.

And if they didn't find Ryan safe and alive, he would blame her in the end just as she blamed herself.

She started to pull away, but he lifted her chin with the pad of his thumb and looked into her eyes. For a moment, she thought she detected something deeper than compassion blazing in his eyes, something akin to desire, as if he found her attractive.

As if he didn't blame her for losing his son, as if he wanted her. Then he angled his head and pressed his lips over hers. Brianna sighed in contentment and allowed him to deepen the kiss.

But Derrick's cell phone buzzed, jarring them both back to the situation. He released her and pulled the phone from the clip at his belt. "Sit down and eat something, Bri. You need to keep up your energy."

Her stomach rumbled, but she wasn't hungry. Still, on rote, she forced down a few bites of the sandwich while he connected the call.

"Yeah. Good. Thanks, Sheriff." He snapped the phone shut, then joined her at the table as if the kiss had never happened. "That was Cramer. He's gotten the go ahead to have Natalie's body exhumed for an autopsy."

Brianna dropped the sandwich on the plate. "I hate to do that, but I guess it's necessary."

Derrick's jaw tightened. "It is if we want to make sure she wasn't murdered."

Brianna remembered Natalie's beautiful face, the tight bond they'd formed as children. She had to find out the truth for Natalie's sake and for her son.

DERRICK PHONED HIS INSURANCE company to report the explosion, then phoned Billy Driscill's house.

A woman answered. "The Driscill residence. This is Alma, his housekeeper, speaking."

"This is Derrick McKinney from Guardian Angel Investigations. I need to speak to Mr. Driscill concerning a criminal matter."

"Mr. Driscill isn't home. May I take a message?"

"This is urgent," Derrick said. "It may have to do with the baby who was kidnapped from Brianna Honeycutt's house."

"Oh, dear, I heard about that. How horrible."

"Then please tell us where we can find Billy Driscill."

"He's at his cabin on the river." She gave him the

address, and Derrick hung up and reached for his jacket. Brianna was already tugging on her coat and gloves. A blanket of snow whitened the ground, but the flurries had ceased for the moment. Still, the cold hit them as they hurried to her car, and the wind sent the trees into a wild flutter. Branches scattered moisture onto the road so he watched for black ice as he drove, slowing around the curves.

The road leading to the cabin was a narrow graveled slit carved through the trees, the old log cabin perched on the edge of the riverbank. Smoke billowed from the chimney, and Derrick spotted a pickup truck in the clearing. He cut the engine, opened the door and rushed around the front to help Brianna, but she was already out.

"What do you think he can tell us?" she asked as they picked their way through the patches of weeds and snow-clumped grounds.

"I don't know. Maybe he had a lead about that hospital explosion, but never had enough evidence to pursue a case." Or maybe he'd known who had done it and covered it up. His son Charlie had always been a golden child, popular and protected by his father who ran the town. Evan Rutherford's parents had owned half of Sanctuary.

And judging from the edge in Gage's voice when they'd discussed the party and that date rape drug, Charlie had had something to feel guilty about or he wouldn't have resigned from office.

Derrick raised his fist and knocked, while Brianna huddled inside her coat, staring at the water racing over the jagged rocks. "It's freezing out here," she whispered. "Surely this man wouldn't be so callous as to abandon Ryan in the elements."

She turned tortured eyes toward him, and he wanted to assure her—and himself—that no one could be that cruel. But the words stuck in his throat, and he couldn't bring himself to lie to her.

People could be that cruel. More cruel than she could possibly imagine.

He'd witnessed the evidence of their brutality on children before. The strangers were difficult to swallow, but the parents—how anyone could hurt their own child never ceased to shock and horrify him.

"Try to hold on to hope." He squeezed her arm. "If he'd killed Ryan, he wouldn't have bothered to leave that note."

Despair filled Brianna's voice. "He could be lying."

The memory of the past taunted him. The sight of that small grave on his last case....

He couldn't bear to see his own son in the ground.

He couldn't deny that she might be right, either.

He knocked again, and this time, shuffling sounded inside.

"Hang on to your britches, I'm coming!" Driscill shouted.

A second later, the door swung open. Derrick had left town years ago, and although Driscill had aged, his hair was graying and thinning, his wrinkles more pronounced, he still had an air of blustery arrogance about him. "What in the hell are you doing up here?"

"My name is Derrick McKinney." He explained he was working with Guardian Angel Investigations. "I'm sure you heard about the missing infant."

Driscill scrubbed his hand over a few days' worth of beard stubble that had collected on his jaw. "Yeah, I heard. But what's that got to do with me?"

"Maybe nothing, but we need to ask you some questions." Brianna's teeth chattered. "May we please come in?"

Brianna's body was tense, but she pasted on a smile, one Derrick realized was her attempt to charm their way inside. Driscill responded automatically, his narrowed eyes softening as he waved for her to enter.

"I have coffee." Driscill gestured toward the kitchen.

"That would be wonderful," Brianna responded. "Thank you so much."

They followed the older man to the kitchen where he filled mugs and placed them on the table. Driscill sat down beside Brianna but faced Derrick.

"How can I help?"

Derrick relayed the details of the case, ending on his conversation with Gage. Anger flashed in Driscill's eyes at the mention of his partner. "What the hell? Is McDermont trying to pin this on me or my son?"

"No." Derrick intentionally used a neutral voice. "Natalie worked at the high school. It appears that she may have known something about a meth lab nearby. One that might be linked to the past and a group called The Club."

Driscill's lips thinned to a straight line. "There were all kinds of clubs in high school."

Derrick bit back his irritation. Driscill was so defensive of his son that he obviously didn't intend to offer any information that might incriminate Charlie.

"We think there may be a connection between Natalie's

death, the kidnapping and the explosion eight years ago that caused the hospital fire. Did you have any leads on that case? Any suspects?"

Driscill took a sip of his coffee as if measuring what to say, but the worry lines around his eyes deepened. "Nothing concrete. But it was the worst thing that ever happened to this town. Everyone in a panic. So many people dead, grown-ups, kids, old people. Everyone throwing blame on everyone else."

"Can you remember anyone specifically who you thought might have been involved?"

He shook his head. "We didn't have a crime scene unit nearby, and by the time the state guys arrived, finding evidence was a mess. Between the rescue workers and the fire, a lot of forensics was destroyed."

"Was there any evidence of a bomb?"

"Not that they discovered. One of the arson investigators said it was some kind of chemical fire, that it might have started in the pharmacy, and ruled it an accident that might have been related to faulty wiring. The hospital paid out their butts in lawsuits, and the director at the time ended up committing suicide. The note said he was haunted by the voices of the dead."

"A chemical fire," Derrick said, his mind racing as a childhood memory surfaced. He had done a project for history one year, a project where he'd had to study the evolution of the town.

"At one time there were tunnels and mines within these mountains, weren't there?"

Driscill cut his eyes toward him. "Yes. Years and years ago."

"But some of them are still accessible?"

"There's been rumors of the homeless living in them during the winters."

"Those underground tunnels would have been a perfect place to hide a meth lab," Derrick said.

Brianna's eyes widened, and Driscill clenched his coffee mug in an iron grip. "You think a meth lab might be responsible for that explosion?"

Derrick shrugged. "It's possible. Think of the chemicals involved, the danger in the enclosed space. There are tunnels below the ground where that hospital was built."

"And Natalie could have learned who was responsible," Brianna commented.

Derrick nodded. "Someone who still lives in Sanctuary. Someone who knows they caused all those deaths."

"Someone who thought Natalie was getting too close," Brianna guessed. "And they had to keep her quiet."

"Just like they wanted to do with us when they set that car explosion." Derrick turned back to Driscill, his silence nagging at him. "Did you know about the meth lab, Driscill?"

"If I had, I would have done something to stop it and arrest whoever caused that explosion."

"Not if your son was involved." Derrick watched the man's face blanch.

Driscill pushed to his feet, the sound of his chair scraping the wood floor. "My son wasn't involved in any such thing. Now I've told you what I know, so I suggest you get the hell out."

HE STARED AT THE CHARRED remains of McKinney's SUV, and cursed. Dammit, he'd wanted the P.I. and that woman to be dead inside. The note had been only for show, to lure them closer to the car.

He had no intention of giving that baby back.

Stupid fools didn't even realize that now. Why did Brianna have to adopt the kid herself? Why couldn't she have let another couple from out of town adopt him? Someone who wouldn't have brought in the baby's father.

Someone who wouldn't have asked questions about Natalie's death.

Someone who wouldn't be stirring up the town now with questions about the past.

A past that needed to stay buried. Exposing the truth after all these years would only cause more pain and heartache to the town. It would tear apart decent people's lives.

His would not be destroyed. He'd kept his secrets too long. He had to do whatever it took to protect himself and his family.

Yes, the Honeycutt woman had to die. And so did McKinney.

Chapter Eleven

Brianna contemplated the former sheriff's reaction as she settled in the car and buckled her seat belt. She remembered Sheriff Driscill as being formidable but friendly, and she'd never had trouble with the law herself. Although he had come to Magnolia Manor a few times when she'd lived there as a teen, it was always to question some boy who he suspected had caused trouble.

Most of the town supported the center for abandoned kids, but there had always been a few who didn't want them around. The ones who were quick to blame any petty crime or problem on the teens they considered delinquents just because they had no family.

"Why do you think he got so angry?" Brianna asked as Derrick drove down the driveway from Billy Driscill's cabin to the highway leading back to Sanctuary.

"Because we hit a nerve. He has always protected his son, and he obviously thought I was trying to implicate Charlie in the explosion."

"Why would he automatically think that?"

Derrick let a half smile slide onto his face. "Because

Charlie is guilty of something, and his father knows it. And he also knows that we're getting closer than he ever did to the truth about that night. Unless…"

"Unless what?"

"Unless Charlie was in this club, and Driscill sabotaged the case or hid evidence to keep his son from going to jail."

"And the town from knowing that he was responsible for all those lost lives." Brianna shuddered. "Do you think that's why Charlie resigned from running for sheriff? That his guilt finally caught up with him?"

"I don't know."

"I can't imagine living with the knowledge that I'd killed innocent people," Brianna said. "Even if it was an accident."

"Well, don't feel sorry for Charlie until we get some answers. He may be responsible for Natalie's death and for Ryan's kidnapping."

The image of Derrick's SUV on fire flashed in her mind, and the sound of the explosion reverberated in her head. "And for nearly killing us."

Derrick took her hand in his. "Hang in there, Bri. We're going to find Ryan. I know we will."

Brianna wrapped her hopes around his words and clung to his hand. She prayed he was right. She missed the feel of the baby in her arms.

Her stomach clenched as her imagination took a fantasy detour, and she imagined holding Ryan with Derrick by her side. The three of them as a family. The family she'd never had.

The family she wanted more than anything.

DERRICK FOUND CHARLIE DRISCILL at the garage where he'd worked since resigning from the sheriff's department. Apparently his hobby had been tinkering with cars and old man Jones had wanted to sell his business and move to Florida because of his arthritis, so Charlie took over the business.

Derrick glanced at Brianna as they walked up to the entrance. "Are you sure you're up to this?"

"Yes."

Her bruises reminded him that beneath that sweater, her ribs must still be aching, but she didn't complain. She held her chin up and followed him inside. The smell of grease, oil and sweat permeated the air. The front desk was unmanned, so he picked his way past stacks of car parts and tires to the garage. The sound of country music wafting from a radio echoed off the cement walls, and a pair of feet protruded from beneath an old Chevy.

"Charlie Driscill," Derrick called. "Charlie, we need to talk to you." He nudged Charlie's feet with his own.

A second later, Charlie rolled from beneath the car, frowning as he peered up at them. "What you need? Work on your car?"

His was too far gone. "No, we need to ask you some questions. It's about the baby kidnapping."

Charlie pushed to his feet. "I'm sorry. I heard about that." He grimaced as he looked at Brianna. "That guy did a number on you, didn't he?"

Brianna touched her cheek self-consciously, and Derrick clamped his jaw tight. "Yeah, he did. And we're trying to find the baby and the man who took him."

"I'm afraid I can't help you," Charlie shrugged. "I'm not the law around here anymore."

"But I think you can help." Derrick produced his ID. "I'm working with Gage McDermont at GAI and I just spoke with your father."

Anger and wariness flashed in Driscill's eyes, then he grabbed the rag attached to his belt and began to wipe his hands. Derrick and Brianna followed him to his office.

"And they told you to talk to me? Why? I didn't have anything to do with a kidnapping."

"It's indirectly related." Derrick summarized the facts he'd unveiled so far, and their speculations about the connection between a current meth lab and one that might have been responsible for the hospital explosion eight years ago.

Driscill frowned and rubbed his chin. "I still don't see how I can help. I didn't do drugs back then and I sure as hell don't now."

"But you were a deputy around here and acting sheriff for a while. Did you ever investigate any kids for drugs, or get wind of a possible meth lab in the area?"

Driscill seemed to think for a minute. "I broke up a couple of kids smoking weed a few times, but never made any arrests. It was petty stuff, and they weren't selling. I let them off with a warning."

"Where was that?"

"Up at Taylor's Ridge. You know how it is. It was just kids' stuff."

"No meth?"

A vein pulsed in Charlie's throat. "No heavy stuff or I would have busted their butts."

"How about eight years ago? The rumor is that there was a club back then, some group that put together a lab."

Driscill stroked his jaw. "There were all kinds of clubs in high school."

"Think, Driscill. I was gone from Sanctuary by then."

"Please, Charlie," Brianna urged softly.

"If Natalie found out about this club and they were responsible for people dying in that hospital fire, one of them might have killed Natalie to keep her quiet."

"Killed Natalie?" Driscill's brows rose. "I thought she died giving birth."

"In light of what's happened," Derrick said, "her body is being exhumed for an autopsy."

Driscill's mouth flattened.

"We know Harry Wiggins brought a date rape drug to the party you guys attended eight years ago, the same night the hospital burned down. Where did he get the drugs?"

The vein in Driscill's neck throbbed again, the wariness in his expression deepening. "I have no idea. That was Harry's doings. He was always a science geek."

Derrick narrowed his eyes as a thought struck him. "A science geek?"

"Yeah, he was only at the party because he brought the drug. We weren't friends."

Derrick nodded. "Maybe Harry and some of his geek friends created the meth lab."

"Harry is dead now," Charlie said gruffly.

Right. So he couldn't have orchestrated the kidnapping. "But if one or more of his friends still live around here, they wouldn't want the truth to be revealed."

"Can you remember who Harry's friends were?" Brianna asked.

A tense hesitation followed.

"Please tell us, Charlie," Brianna whispered. "Whoever did this may have Ryan. And if he killed Natalie and tried to kill me and Derrick, there's no telling what he might do to the baby."

Charlie's face softened at her plea. "Some guy named Wilbur Irkman," he declared. "He's the only one I remember. The guy went to college, but his mother was ill and he moved back to take care of her. I think he's some kind of pharmaceutical rep now."

Derrick nodded and jotted his name in his notepad. A pharmaceutical rep would certainly know a lot about drugs.

Legal ones and illegal.

"I KNOW WILBUR," BRIANNA SAID as they drove toward Irkman's house. "He was valedictorian, always won the science fairs and earned a full ride to UNC."

"Which he didn't deserve if he was responsible for that explosion and those deaths," Derrick commented.

Brianna sighed. "But Wilbur was too thin to be the man who kidnapped Ryan."

"He could have hired someone else to. The entire club could have orchestrated this together to cover themselves."

Brianna turned to stare out the window. The daylight was waning, the dark storm clouds casting a dismal gray across the mountains. The temperature was dropping again, the wind rattling the trees.

Her heart clenched. Babies couldn't talk but they formed bonds with people, and Ryan had bonded with her. He must sense that she wasn't around, could smell the difference between her and this stranger.

Would they hold him and comfort him when he cried?

"Did Irkman ever marry?" Derrick asked.

Brianna forced herself to focus although the thought of Ryan crying for her made her sick inside. "No."

"Do you remember any of his friends?"

"No," Brianna answered. "Between working as a cashier at the grocery store and taking care of the younger kids at Magnolia Manor, I was too busy to have a lot of friends."

Derrick's jaw tightened. "You were saving money for college?"

Memories of wondering if she'd ever make it to college surfaced, along with her own bitterness over being abandoned. A bitterness she'd struggled to put behind her. A bitterness which had helped her understand other children and drove her to help them.

"I had to," she murmured. "I didn't want to end up in a dead-end job like...my mother." Or turning to hooking and drugs as she had.

No, she would never have done that.

And she would never have abandoned a child.

Derrick gave her an odd look, and she clamped her lip with her teeth. She'd never shared her feelings with anyone but Natalie. Telling Derrick made her feel vulnerable.

Wilbur's subdivision appeared in her vision, and Derrick turned onto the street. The houses had been built over fifty years ago, and were a mixture of brick ranches and split-levels. Wilbur lived in a red split-level with a barn-like roof.

The house badly needed paint, and a rusted sedan sat under a carport. Snow weighed down the branches of the trees and covered the roof. The only Christmas decorations in sight consisted of a red bow on the mailbox and a lopsided wreath on the front door. No twinkling lights, and from the front window, no evidence of a tree.

Derrick parked behind the sedan and they rushed through the cold to the front door. Brianna paced while Derrick punched the doorbell. She silently prayed Wilbur was home and had some answers that would lead them to Ryan.

She wanted the baby home for the holidays, to see his little eyes brighten as he watched the Christmas tree lights dance in the room.

She wanted to hold him and love him and never let him go.

The door opened, and a frail-looking woman in a tattered housecoat leaned against the doorjamb. Her graying hair was thinning, her pallor a chalky white, her slight frame trembling as if she was barely hanging on to life.

"Mrs. Irkman," Derrick began. "My name is Derrick McKinney with Guardian Angel Investigations and this is Brianna Honeycutt."

Her brown eyes pierced Brianna. "You the one with the kidnapped baby?"

"Yes, ma'am," Brianna answered gently. "We need to talk to your son Wilbur."

"Wilbur ain't here," she said, then broke into a cough.

Derrick jammed his hands in his pockets. "May we come in, ma'am? I'd like to ask you some questions."

Suspicion laced her eyes. "What about?"

"We know that Wilbur hung around with Harry Wiggins in high school. Were they still friends?" Derrick asked.

"How can they be friends when Harry is dead?"

"I meant in the last few years," Derrick clarified.

"Harry never came around," she said sharply. "And rightly so. That boy kidnapped Ruby Holden last year." As if she suddenly realized the connection they might have seen, she clacked her teeth. "My son don't know anything about your baby being missing."

"Where is he now?" Derrick inquired.

"Out of town on business. Had to go up to the Research Triangle Park."

Derrick folded his arms. "When will he be back?"

She frowned. "Tomorrow. I got a doctor's appointment, and he promised to take me." Her look softened. "That boy has been good to me. He moved back to take care of me, you know."

"That's nice of him," Brianna told her, sympathy welling in her chest. Still, if Wilbur had had something to do with that explosion or Ryan being kidnapped, they had to know.

"Let me ask you one more thing," Derrick prodded. "Eight years ago, some boys around here had a club. We think they started a meth lab below the hospital and that it exploded and caused that hospital fire."

Mrs. Irkman's eyes widened in her gaunt face. "What are you saying? That my boy was involved with that?"

"Was he?" Derrick asked.

"Of course not. Wilbur was valedictorian. He went to UNC, and he's got a fine job now. He was not into drugs back then or now."

"Mrs. Irkman," Brianna interjected, reaching out to calm her.

But the older woman shook her hand off and reached for the door. "Get out of here, Mr. McKinney, and don't you bother to come back."

Brianna jumped back and Derrick glowered at the woman as she slammed the door in their face.

Brianna hugged her arms around her middle as they rushed back to the car. Mrs. Irkman might be seriously ill, but she had enough strength to slam her door. Was her anger a normal parental protective response, or was she hiding something?

DERRICK'S PHONE VIBRATED AS HE started the engine and pulled away from the Irkman house. He quickly glanced at the number. Ben, GAI.

Maybe they had a lead from the Amber Alert.

Hissing out a breath, he connected the call. "McKinney speaking."

"Derrick, I have news."

"You found Ryan?"

"No, man, I'm sorry. Not yet."

Disappointment ballooned in his chest. "Then what is it?"

Ben cleared his throat. "The results of the paternity tests are in."

Chapter Twelve

Derrick held his breath as he maneuvered the turn, his pulse pounding as he waited on the answer to the paternity test. He'd already begun to think of Ryan as his son. Yet he had no idea how to be a father.

And if Ryan wasn't his, then he'd have no ties. No ties to the child or Brianna.

His chest throbbed at the thought.

"Derrick, are you there?" Ben asked.

Derrick scrubbed his hand over his face. "Yeah. What are the results?"

"You are Ryan's father, Derrick. There's no doubt."

The air left Derrick's lungs in a mad rush. The image of the little blond baby in the photos at Brianna's house flashed into his mind. Ryan was his son.

Yet he hadn't been there for his birth, hadn't held him once.

He had to get him back. Had to make it up to him.

"Thanks," he managed to say on a choked breath.

"No problem. I'll keep you posted if we get a lead." The line went dead, and Derrick snapped his phone closed.

"Was that news about Ryan?" Brianna asked, an edge of hope amid desperation in her voice.

He gave a clipped nod. "Yes. But no lead on the kidnapper or his location."

"Then what?"

He wasn't sure how Brianna was going to react.

"The results of the paternity test came in."

Brianna twisted her hands together. "Ryan is yours, isn't he?"

"Yes." Derrick gritted his teeth. "You knew all along that Natalie had lied to me, didn't you?"

She shook her head. "She lied to me, too, Derrick."

"But you suspected the truth?"

"Only when I saw him. There was something about his eyes and his hair that made me wonder."

Anger and hurt suffused him, and he steered the car to a clearing by the river and screeched to a stop. "Then why didn't you tell me? Because you didn't think I was father material?"

BRIANNA FLINCHED AT THE ANGER lacing Derrick's tone.

"Why didn't you tell me?" He gripped her arms. "Because of my reputation years ago? Or you heard about the case I screwed up and didn't think I deserved a son?"

"What?" Brianna's eyes widened. "No, Derrick. I never meant to keep the truth from you. I was only trying to do what Natalie asked of me. I had to keep my promise to her, and then…"

"Then what?" he asked harshly.

"And then I fell in love with Ryan." And she hadn't wanted to lose him.

Shame filled her along with regret and fear. Judging from the anguish on Derrick's face, she'd hurt him. Because she'd been selfish and had worried that he'd want to take Ryan away from her.

He released her abruptly, then pressed both of his hands over his face and inhaled sharply. "God… I'm sorry. You're right. I don't deserve a son."

Brianna's heart clenched. "That's not true, Derrick. And that's not the reason I didn't contact you. I honestly didn't know Ryan was yours. In fact, I hoped he wasn't."

A cold rage seared his eyes as he looked back at her. "I see. Then I was right. You didn't think I would make a good father. I let one child die and you didn't trust me with Ryan."

Brianna reached for his arm. She had to convince him that wasn't true. But how could she without revealing the entire truth, that she'd fudged papers to make sure Ryan was hers legally. And if that reality aired, she'd not only lose Ryan but she'd lose her job.

"You keep talking about that last case." Brianna recognized the guilt that was eating him alive. "What happened?"

He virtually shut down in front of her, the pain in his eyes turning cold, his body becoming rigid. "I trusted the wrong person, the mother," he said bluntly.

Without another word, he started the engine and sped back onto the highway, his words echoing in her ears. *He'd trusted the wrong person, the mother.*

But that mother had obviously lied to him.

And he'd trusted that Natalie would've told him about his son and she'd lied, too.

No wonder he was enraged at Natalie and her. And if he discovered that she'd fudged those papers, he'd hate her.

She twisted her fingers together, her heart pounding. She didn't want to lose Ryan.

But she didn't want Derrick to hate her, either.

"Derrick—"

"Don't say anything else, Brianna," he muttered. "I have to focus on finding Ryan. I won't let the same thing that happened to that other child happen to my son."

DERRICK CLAMPED HIS MOUTH shut, self-recriminations echoing in his head. His bad-boy reputation in high school had been infamous. He'd carried a weight of anger around with him, anger that had landed him in trouble.

Anger at his father for the beatings and for making him feel worthless as hell.

When his old man had drunk himself into the grave, and he'd left Sanctuary, he'd tried to channel that anger into saving innocent victims.

And then that child's death...

How could he blame Brianna and Natalie for not trusting him with his son? Everyone in town knew his father's reputation. They might have feared he'd be like his old man.

But he would prove them wrong. If—no, *when*—he got Ryan back, he would never harm a hair on his kid's head.

His phone buzzed, slicing through the tension-laden air. Hoping for a lead, he connected the call.

"Mr. McKinney?"

"Yes?"

"This is Evan Rutherford, the coach at the high

school. I heard you were looking into a possible meth lab run by some teenagers."

Derrick shifted, focused now. "Yes. Do you know something that could help?"

"I'm not trying to pin it on anyone, but there's a kid who might have some information."

"What's his name?"

"Ace Atkins, he lives over at Magnolia Manor. He's a real tough guy with a chip on his shoulder a mile high."

"What makes you think he might be involved?"

"I don't know for sure. Just a hunch. The crowd he hangs with is rough."

Derrick gritted his teeth. He had a kinship with the kid. He'd hung with the wrong crowd in school, too. And he'd caught the brunt of the suspicions any time trouble occurred in town, guilty or not. "Thanks. I'll have a talk with him."

Rutherford started to hang up, but Derrick caught him. "Listen, Rutherford. You were in the same class as Harry Wiggins, Gage McDermont and Charlie Driscill." He went on to describe his suspicions about the hospital explosion. "Charlie said that Harry brought the drugs and told me to talk to Wilbur Irkman, that he might have known about a meth lab back then. Can you fill in any of the blanks?"

A moment of silence, then Evan cleared his throat. "I do remember those science geeks. Irkman hung out with another guy named Mark Larimer. I think he's a nurse at the local hospital now."

"Thanks. I'll check into Larimer. And if you hear anything else around the school, let me know."

Evan agreed, and Derrick disconnected the call.

"What was that about?" Brianna asked.

"We're going to Magnolia Manor to talk to a kid Evan Rutherford said might know something about the meth lab."

"Who?" Brianna asked.

"A kid named Ace."

Brianna sighed. "He has been trouble."

They fell into a strained silence as he steered the car toward the orphanage where Brianna had grown up.

Ten minutes later, they parked at the two-story Victorian house. Brianna seemed quiet, almost withdrawn as they entered, and he regretted his earlier outburst. Had he frightened her when he'd grabbed her arms?

A young woman in her early thirties greeted Brianna with a smile, her demeanor indicating they'd met before. "Bri, I'm so sorry to hear about Ryan. Is there any word?"

"That's why we're here, Rachel." She introduced her to Derrick, saying that Rachel was a counselor at the manor. Derrick let her take the lead and explain why they were there.

Meanwhile he studied the house. A Christmas tree had been decorated in the den with presents already wrapped beneath, a garland was strung along the staircase, wreaths on the walls. Upstairs he heard voices and laughter, and the scent of homemade cookies filled the air.

It seemed more like a home than an orphanage, and had obviously been renovated inside and out. From the stories he'd heard when he was young, it hadn't always been a nice place to live.

Brianna sighed. "We think this meth lab might be

connected to one eight years ago that caused a terrible explosion in town."

Rachel's green eyes flickered with worry. "Bri, I know Ace has an attitude, but I don't think he's involved with drugs. I've been counseling him for the past few months, and he seems clean."

"Even so, he might know something," Derrick said. "Is he here?"

"No, he goes by the community center to play basketball after school. He should be there now."

Derrick turned to Brianna. "You can stay here if you want, but I'm going to talk to him."

Brianna shook her head. "No, I want to be there."

He frowned at her tone, wondering if she didn't trust him with the young man. What did she think he would do—try to beat the truth out of him?

Fresh snowflakes fluttered to the ground as they rode in silence to the community center. "When did they build this?" Derrick asked as they walked up the sidewalk to the entrance.

"About five years ago," Brianna said. "I think the community needed it. They have a gym, workout room, rec room with big screen TVs, Ping-Pong tables and other games as well as a concession stand. Volunteers from the town help man it so they can keep it open on weekend nights for kids to hang out."

He nodded, wondering if he'd had a place like this as a teen if he would have taken advantage of it. Doing so might have kept him out of trouble.

Contemporary funky furniture created cozy nooks for hanging out. Several kids were seated on cushions watching movies while others played video games. Another group of middle schoolers were playing Twister while a corner held instruments for the kids to jam.

"The gym is this way," Brianna said and led him through a set of double doors down a hall to the gym. A dozen or so boys were playing basketball, while a small group of girls watched with starry eyes.

"Ace Atkins," Derrick called out.

A black-haired muscular kid who'd been dribbling the ball paused and looked at him. "Who's asking?"

Brianna touched Derrick's arm, signaling for him to let her speak up. "Ace, may we talk to you, please? It's important."

Ace stared at her for a long minute, then nodded and passed the ball to another boy. The game continued as he strode toward them, his tough-boy attitude evident in his eyes.

He crossed his arms, automatically defensive as he met them by the stands. "What's up?"

"Ace, you heard about the baby I adopted being kidnapped?"

He shifted, then picked at something on his athletic shorts. "Yeah. But I ain't got nothin' to do with that."

"I'm not saying you did," Brianna spoke softly. "But this is the baby's father, Derrick McKinney. He's also working with Guardian Angel Investigations and the sheriff to help me find Ryan."

Ace shrugged, his gaze full of distrust as he glanced at Derrick. Derrick understood too well his reaction. He'd been on the other end of this sort of conversation years ago. Once he'd earned a bad reputation, the teachers and authorities had tried to pin any vandalism or petty crime on him.

"Look, Ace," Derrick cut in. "We have reason to believe that the baby's mother, Ms. Cummings who taught at your school, might have uncovered a meth lab nearby. Do you know anything about it?"

Ace cursed. "Just 'cause I live at the manor, you think I'm into drugs. That ain't fair, man."

"We're not accusing you," Brianna stated. "But maybe you overheard some other kids talking about the lab. Please, Ace. It might have something to do with finding Ryan." She gave him an imploring look. "He's just a few weeks old, Ace. He's not strong and tough like you. He can't defend himself, and he might be in danger."

Derrick heard the pain in Brianna's plea and saw Ace responding with a change in attitude. He relaxed his shoulders, then leaned closer to Brianna and lowered his voice. "Then instead of lookin' at me, you ought to talk to Jeremy Dahl."

"Who is he?" Derrick asked.

A smirk slid onto Ace's face. "The big jock in school, the golden boy. The one no one would think to ask. He's probably at practice now."

Derrick's cell phone buzzed, and he checked the caller ID. Sheriff Cramer.

"I have to answer this." He thanked the young boy and walked away to connect the call. "McKinney speaking."

"It's Cramer. I just talked to the medical examiner."

Derrick gripped the phone with sweaty fingers. "And?"

"It looks like you were right, McKinney. Natalie didn't die of natural causes. She was murdered."

Chapter Thirteen

Brianna's chest clenched at the look of anger on Derrick's face.

"We'll meet you at the hospital in an hour." Derrick disconnected and closed his phone.

"What's wrong, Derrick? Was that about Ryan?"

"No," he answered in a gruff voice. His eyes were tortured as he looked at her. "That was the sheriff. He talked to the medical examiner and we were right. Natalie was murdered."

Brianna gasped. Even though they'd suspected it, hearing the reality hit her hard. "How?"

"Apparently she was injected with a drug that induced heart failure."

"Who would do such a horrible thing?" Brianna whispered.

"Someone who wanted to keep her quiet," Derrick said. "Do you remember seeing anyone suspicious that night?"

Brianna massaged her temple, struggling to think back. "It was so chaotic," she recalled in a low voice.

"Natalie was frightened, and I was trying to calm her and help her inside."

A muscle jumped in Derrick's jaw, and Brianna realized how difficult this must be for him.

"What else do you remember?"

"An orderly and nurse assisted Natalie inside. They whisked her to the E.R. I wanted to go with her, but they said they needed to check her over, then I could."

"And did you?"

"No. I waited and waited." She twisted her hands together. "Then I got nervous so I asked a nurse. She said there were complications, that they had to do an emergency C-section."

"Did you see anyone in the waiting room who looked suspicious? Maybe someone who came into the E.R. after you?"

She closed her eyes, mentally reliving that night, but nothing came to mind. Nothing except the fear that had made her heart pound. "Not that I remember." She glanced up at him. "God, Derrick. Why wasn't I more observant? I should have insisted on going to the exam room with Natalie. Labor coaches and partners go into the E.R. for C-sections these days, but I trusted them."

Tears filled her eyes. "If I had been with her, Natalie might still be alive."

"Dammit, Bri. This is not your fault." Hating the look of guilt haunting her eyes, Derrick reached out and pressed his hand over hers. "I'm Ryan's father. I should have been there." He hesitated and swallowed hard. "If

Natalie had told me about Ryan I would have been. Then I could have protected her and the baby and none of this would have happened."

"Derrick—"

"No, Bri. It's true and you know it. If Natalie had trusted me, had thought I was father material, she would have told me. She might have even confided what had frightened her, and I could have stopped these maniacs from kidnapping my son."

Guilt clawed at him, guilt mixed with anger over the fact that Natalie had kept his son from him.

That he might not be able to make it up to Ryan for Natalie being murdered and leaving him without a mother.

Except Brianna had filled that role. She obviously loved Ryan as if he was her son.

So why wasn't Brianna blaming him?

Because she'd known the truth all along?

She'd denied it, but she could have lied just as that woman in his last case had.

Confusion muddled his brain, panic over where his son was making his throat tight.

"It's not your fault, either," Brianna said in a choked whisper.

Derrick used to shut down when he was a kid, when his father had drowned himself in booze and started the beatings. He'd refused to allow his father to see his fear.

Or his pain.

He wouldn't now. He hadn't found Ryan yet. And he owed it to Natalie to bring him home.

"I told Cramer we'd meet him at the hospital in an

hour. Let's go talk to Jeremy Dahl." Clamping his jaw tight, he started the engine and headed to the high school.

"Did you believe Ace?" Brianna said as he drove through town.

"I'm on the fence."

"He's had a tough life," Brianna noted, her tone defensive. "His father abused him for years and now he's in the orphanage."

Derrick cut his eyes toward her. "Your mother left you and you don't have a chip on your shoulder."

Pain flickered in Brianna's eyes. He hated that he'd put it there.

"I did for a while," she whispered so softly that he almost didn't hear.

Her admission cost him, made him want to stop and pull her into his arms. Made him realize that she wore a strong face, but inside, she'd been hurting for years.

"What happened to change that?" he asked, needing to know for himself. Maybe he could take some lessons from her.

A faraway look settled in her eyes. "I realized that if I didn't want to become like my mother, I had to let go of the anger. That I could help others and make my life what I wanted."

"You would never have been like your mother," he commented, then realized his slip when her face flamed with embarrassment.

"I always feared people knew she was a hooker," Brianna conceded, then turned to look out the window.

He hated himself for making her more uncomfortable and pulled her hand in his. "Brianna, everyone may have known. But I admired you because you worked so hard to improve your life. I did the opposite. I did my best to prove my old man right."

Brianna clenched his hand. "What do you mean? To prove him right?"

"When he beat me, he used to tell me that I wasn't worth spit. After a while, I believed him."

"He lied," Brianna said, then squeezed his hand. "I always thought you were special."

Derrick's gaze caught hers, the tension rippling between them, his chest swelling with her words. Natalie had written that Bri had a crush on him.

Had that been true?

And why had she? He'd been a troubled kid with the law on his tail.

Disturbed by his reaction to her, Derrick jerked his attention back to the road and pulled into the high school parking lot. But the bitter memories taunted him, crowding his mind with regret and guilt. One memory in particular—the day he'd been arrested in front of the kids in the gym.

Had Brianna witnessed that? Had Natalie? Was that the reason Natalie had kept the truth about Ryan from him?

What would his son think about the man he'd been?

He'd tried to atone for his past by saving other kids but he'd failed the last one. And now his son...

No, he couldn't fail him now.

BRIANNA BIT HER LIP to keep from saying more to Derrick as he parked. Fool that she was, she'd almost confessed that she'd always wanted him.

And that she wanted him now.

She admired the strong, serious, brooding, protective man he'd become. The man who cared about others, who worked to save children, who'd taken care of her when she'd first been hurt by the kidnapper and hadn't left her side since.

The man who still turned her heart inside out, and made her body tingle with desire. Just the sound of his gruff voice sent an aching chill of need through her.

And when he'd admitted that this father had hurt him, she'd nearly broken down and cried.

And pulled him into her arms.

She tugged her coat closer as they wove their way up the sidewalk to the school. Derrick headed straight to the gym and she followed. They found Coach Rutherford there watching as his team ran laps. Derrick strode over to him, and Brianna joined them, watching Evan's face contort with confusion, questions, then worry as he called a young man over to speak to them.

"Jeremy, this is Derrick McKinney and Brianna Honeycutt," Evan said. "They need to ask you some questions about a meth lab in the area."

Jeremy was a good-looking guy with linebacker shoulders. He wiped sweat from his brow with the back of his hand. "What are you talking about, Coach?"

Derrick told him about the lab and its possible correlation to Natalie's death. "She was your teacher?" Derrick confirmed.

"Yeah, but I didn't hurt her," Jeremy answered. "I liked Ms. Cummings. I mean for a teacher she was okay."

"Do you know any kids involved in drugs in the school?" Derrick asked.

Jeremy shrugged. "A few dopers, but they're not athletes, so we don't hang out."

Evan shook his head. "If you do know something else, spill it now. If you don't, you can be held accountable as an accessory."

"Hey, no fair." Jeremy crossed his arms. "I told you I'm not a doper, and I'm not."

Derrick narrowed his eyes. "Then who is?"

"Talk to that cretin Ace."

"Funny," Derrick said sarcastically, "but he said to talk to you."

Jeremy muttered an ugly word. "Well, he's lying."

"Then give us another name," Derrick pressed.

Jeremy shrugged. "If you wanna find drugs, look at the science club. Talk is, they'd know how to cook up meth."

Brianna's mind raced. The science club—Charlie had mentioned something about some science geeks eight years ago. What if the science club was *The Club* Natalie had discovered, the ones who'd burned down the hospital?

DERRICK SPOTTED SHERIFF Cramer's marked car when he parked at the hospital. Night was falling, daylight dwindling, the strain wearing on him.

The kidnapper could be anywhere by now. Or he could have done something horrible to Ryan and left him God knows where. The woods, a Dumpster...

No, he couldn't think like that. He especially couldn't let Brianna see his fears.

"Did you believe Jeremy Dahl?" Brianna asked as they walked up to the hospital entrance and hurried inside.

Derrick shrugged. "I don't know. He could have been trying to divert suspicion from himself by sending us somewhere else."

She nodded. "We still need to talk to Mark Larimer, too."

"Yeah. We will after we talk to the doctor. And I want to look at a high school yearbook from eight years ago. See who belonged to that science club."

"I have one at home," Brianna offered.

He nodded, and they rode the elevator to the second floor, then walked down the hall to the hospital director's office. Cramer was waiting in the receptionist's office, so they joined him, and a minute later, Sheldon Lake, the director, a forty-something man with a bad toupee and square black-framed glasses, invited them inside.

Derrick let the sheriff explain the reason for their visit.

Lake's reaction was just as Derrick expected. A professional mask, shock at the autopsy report and defensiveness. "I can assure you that none of the hospital staff was involved in Ms. Cummings's death."

Cramer crossed his arms. "Her death occurred in your facility after a procedure one of your doctors performed. And the drug she was given killed her."

"That drug must have been administered by mistake," Dr. Lake argued.

"We need to speak to Dr. Thorpe, the ob-gyn who delivered Ryan," Derrick said. "And we'll need to look at your security tapes from that night."

Lake's face turned pinched, but he pushed his intercom button and asked his receptionist to page Dr. Thorpe, then to contact the chief of security to come to his office.

"Why would you think someone would want to kill Ms. Cummings?" Dr. Lake asked.

Cramer and Derrick exchanged looks, then Cramer spoke up. "We have a possible motive, but the investigation is ongoing."

"Were you working at the hospital when it burned down eight years ago?" Derrick continued.

Lake swiped a hand across his forehead where a bead of perspiration had formed. "Yes. I was in the E.R. back then. It was horrible."

"We suspect that a meth lab might have been built below the facility," Derrick said. "That it might have caused the explosion."

Lake's eyes widened. "Good God. Do you know who was responsible?"

"No, but we think Ms. Cummings might have stumbled on the truth."

Shock strained Lake's features. "And that person killed her?"

"It's a theory," Cramer said.

"Then I'll do everything I can to help you. So many people in town lost loved ones that night. They deserve justice."

A knock sounded, and Dr. Thorpe poked his head in. "You paged me, Dr. Lake?"

"Yes, come in."

Thorpe stiffened as he spotted the sheriff, then his

gaze rested on Brianna and his eyebrows rose. "What's going on, Dr. Lake?"

"Sit down, Dr. Thorpe. I'll explain when our security chief arrives."

A tense silence fell between them, and Thorpe studied Brianna with narrowed eyes as if he already knew her suspicions.

Was he hiding something?

Chapter Fourteen

A chill slid up Brianna's spine at the piercing look in Dr. Thorpe's eyes. She jerked her gaze away, but still felt him watching her. They needed answers and she refused to let him intimidate her.

It seemed like hours, but the security chief finally appeared, a lanky young guy in his twenties named Butch Martin. Dr. Lake directed him to sit down, then steepled his hands on his desk.

"Dr. Thorpe, Butch, we seem to have a problem." Lake gestured toward the sheriff. "Sheriff Cramer has brought something to my attention and we need to get to the bottom of it. Apparently he had Natalie Cummings's body exhumed and the medical examiner performed an autopsy."

Dr. Thorpe's face paled slightly.

"Natalie Cummings didn't die of natural causes as you said," the sheriff countered. "She was given a lethal dose of cocaine. Couple that with her heart murmur, and it caused her to go into cardiac arrest."

"Cocaine, my God." Dr. Thorpe gripped the sides of

his chair. "I would never administer that to a patient with a heart murmur."

Dr. Lake cleared his throat. "Why didn't you order an autopsy?"

Dr. Thorpe's eyes shifted sideways. "I didn't see the point. It presented itself as a heart attack and, with her predisposition and the stress and complications of labor, I thought it was one of those fluke cases." Sweat beaded on his skin. "I still don't see how it's possible that she was murdered."

"Tell us exactly what happened," Dr. Lake prodded.

Dr. Thorpe tapped his fingers on the arm of the chair. "She had trouble delivering. The baby wouldn't drop. He was breach, so we rushed her into surgery. She made it through the C-section, then we finished up and she was wheeled to recovery."

"So she wasn't in distress when she went to recovery?" Derrick summarized.

"No, she was fine." Thorpe drummed his fingers again. "Then one of the nurses beeped me that she'd gone into heart failure. I performed CPR and used the crash cart, but I couldn't save her."

The rush of grief she'd felt when Dr. Thorpe had first told her about Natalie gnawed at her again. "Who was in the recovery room with her?" Brianna asked.

A vein throbbed in his neck. "A team of nurses monitor the recovery room. I don't remember exactly who was on duty that night, but the hospital should have a record."

"Which nurse discovered Natalie was in trouble?" Derrick asked.

"Janie Wilkins," Thorpe said. "She's one of our best."

Sheriff Cramer hooked his thumbs in his belt loops. "We'll need to speak with her."

Dr. Lake buzzed his receptionist again, learned that Janie wouldn't be in for another hour, then left a message for her to report to him when she arrived.

He turned to the security chief. "Let's go to your office. I want you to pull up those tapes of that night so we can review them."

Brianna stood and they followed the security chief to his office. The Christmas garland draped around the doorway mocked her. This Christmas season would haunt her forever.

She braced herself as they entered, anxiety and hope warring within her. She wanted to know who had killed her best friend and left Ryan motherless.

But how could she stand to actually watch her friend being murdered?

DERRICK SAW THE TENSION ON Brianna's face and realized how personal this was for her. Natalie had been her best friend, the one person she'd loved since she was a child.

Not that seeing Natalie murdered wouldn't bother him, but he had seen death before. Cruel, brutal death that had robbed young children of their lives. Deaths that had hardened him. Or so he'd thought.

But Brianna's anguish and the idea of his own son being hurt clawed at his self-control.

Dammit, he had to care about his own son. He'd be a monster like some of the people he'd chased and arrested if he didn't.

But he didn't want to care about Brianna.

Still, he touched her arm and spoke softly. "Bri, why don't you wait outside? If we find this person on tape, it's not going to be easy to watch."

Her gaze locked with his for a moment, and gratitude flashed in her eyes. But she surprised him by shaking her head. "No, I have to follow this through."

The security chief gestured for them to sit down and they gathered in hardback chairs around the array of screens connected to cameras scattered throughout the hospital. He shuffled through the stored tapes and located the one stamped with the date of Natalie's delivery, then fed it into the system. They spent the next few minutes scrolling through the tape, studying the scene where Brianna had driven up with Natalie, the nurses helping her inside and wheeling her to the E.R.

Derrick's jaw clenched at the look of panic on Natalie's face. Brianna had been right—Natalie had been afraid. But he could easily see why she would have dismissed that fear as worry over labor.

Guilt assaulted him again. If he'd been there, maybe things would have been different. He narrowed his eyes, searching for anyone suspicious who might have followed Natalie and Brianna inside, but saw nothing. Just a couple of patients being brought in. A man with a child. A woman with her mother.

"Do you have feed in the exam room?" Derrick asked.

"No, the exam rooms aren't monitored to protect the patients' privacy. But the halls and corridors and elevators are."

Derrick watched Brianna pacing the waiting room,

then time lapsed, and Dr. Thorpe came out to break the news that Natalie had died.

"Let's see the surgery," Dr. Lake requested.

Butch scrolled through until he found the clip, and they watched as Natalie was rolled into surgery. She was alert, frightened-looking, but the anesthesiologist gave her an epidural and soothed her nerves, then Dr. Thorpe raised the scalpel.

Derrick had missed being there when his son was born, but emotions clogged his throat as the doctor lifted the baby from Natalie's womb. Tears of joy flowed down Natalie's cheeks as they quickly examined the baby, cleaned him, wrapped him in a blue blanket and handed him to her. Nuzzling the baby to her, she whispered her love.

"She did get to hold him," Brianna said softly. "I had wondered if she did."

Derrick glanced sideways and saw the tears swimming in her eyes. He had to look away so he wouldn't pull her into his arms and comfort her.

The next few minutes passed as Dr. Thorpe finished with Natalie, but just as he'd claimed, Natalie was alert and even smiling as they moved her to the recovery room.

"See, I told you she was fine." Dr. Thorpe gestured toward the tape.

"Scan the halls and corridors between recovery," Sheriff Cramer ordered.

Butch did as requested, but Derrick saw no one suspicious entering or leaving, only medical personnel. Then for a fraction of a second, the camera blanked out.

"What was that?" Dr. Lake inquired.

"I don't know," Butch said. "Sometimes when the power flicks off, the cameras lose a few moments until the backup generator kicks in."

"Did you lose power that night?" Derrick questioned.

Butch shook his head. "Not that I remember." He glanced at Dr. Thorpe.

"No," Thorpe agreed.

The camera flashed back on and caught the image of a figure clad in surgical garb exiting the recovery room. Derrick glanced at Thorpe but the man in the video appeared taller than the ob-gyn.

"That's him," Derrick confirmed. "Whoever killed Natalie disguised himself as a doctor. That's why no one saw him or thought he was suspicious." He frowned up at Thorpe and Dr. Lake. "That is, unless he's really on staff here."

"You're crazy," Dr. Thorpe said. "No one in this hospital would hurt a patient."

"Pull all the employee records," Sheriff Cramer said. "I'll need to look over them, anyway."

Derrick shot him a look of approval. "I want to send this tape to GAI. The tech team can enlarge it and get a better look at the man's face."

Dr. Lake's cell phone rang, and he connected the call. "All right, tell Janie to come to the chief security office immediately."

He disconnected and drummed his fingers on the chair edge just as Dr. Thorpe had done in his office earlier. A tense silence vibrated through the room, the tapes only creating more questions.

Five minutes later, Nurse Wilkins appeared, her brows pinched. "Dr. Lake, Dr. Thorpe. What's going on?"

Dr. Lake recapped the circumstances.

"Oh, my God," Janie gasped. "That poor woman was murdered. How in the world did that happen here?"

Cramer gestured to the tape. "Just watch."

Janie patted strands of her hair back into its bun as she watched, then leaned forward with a frown when she saw the man in the surgical garb leaving the recovery room. "Oh, God, that was only a few minutes before I discovered Natalie in cardiac arrest."

"Do you know who that man is?" Dr. Thorpe asked.

Janie shook her head. "No. I don't recognize him but I can't see his face."

"No other surgeons would have been in recovery?" Sheriff Cramer asked.

"Not in labor and delivery," Janie said. "Just the team of nurses. And there was only one other delivery that night."

"How many nurses worked recovery?" Derrick asked.

"Two of us," Janie said. "Myself and Mark Larimer."

Derrick grimaced. Larimer's name again.

"We need to talk to him," Sheriff Cramer said.

She nodded. "Mark's here now. He'll be off duty soon so you need to catch him before he goes home."

Derrick stood abruptly. "Send a copy of that tape to GAI."

"I'll send it to our crime lab," Cramer said.

Derrick and he exchanged wary looks, but Derrick finally conceded. "Just don't let anything happen to it. We'll need it for evidence."

Cramer glared at him but nodded.

Now he definitely wanted to talk to Larimer. He was one of the science geeks eight years ago. One of the guys he suspected might have caused the hospital explosion.

The fact that he worked at the hospital seemed too coincidental.

And he didn't like coincidences.

BRIANNA'S EMOTIONS BOUNCED all over the place as they went to meet Mark Larimer. Seeing Natalie deliver Ryan had touched her heart.

And seeing the expression on Derrick's face had moved her even more. It was obvious how much he loved Ryan and that Natalie's death affected him. But she had no idea how to comfort him because they couldn't bring Natalie back.

She would give up Ryan without a battle once they found him. Ryan deserved to have his father.

She only wished she could be a part of that family, but she could never fill Natalie's shoes.

Oh, Natalie, why didn't you come to Derrick or me? We would have helped you.

She should have pushed Natalie to confide in her those last few weeks. They could have gone to the sheriff and gotten help.

Why hadn't Natalie confided in Beau?

Because she'd been afraid for herself and her baby.

Janie and Dr. Thorpe returned to work, so Dr. Lake led them to the nurses' station where he asked for Mark.

The nurse nodded, then went to find Mark. A few

seconds later, she returned, a thin guy with curly brown hair, wire-rimmed glasses and a goatee behind her.

"Mark, let's go the break room," Dr. Lake said. "We need to talk."

Alarm flashed in Mark's eyes, but he gave a jerky nod and they all retreated into a small room containing sofas, chairs and tables, a microwave, refrigerator and coffeepot. At Dr. Lake's gesture, they seated themselves around one of the round tables.

"What's going on?" Mark twisted his hands together in his lap, but not before Brianna noted that he'd chewed his nails down to the quick.

Mark's eyes were two different colors, one pale green, the other hazel. Brianna shifted as he flicked them around the table as if he was dissecting them under a microscope.

"Did you know Natalie Cummings?" Derrick began.

Mark shook his head. "Who?"

"She taught at the high school," Brianna explained.

"She also attended high school with you, Mark," Derrick elaborated. "She was a couple of years younger."

Mark shrugged. "I wasn't into girls back then."

Derrick raised a brow. "You mean they weren't into you. Didn't you belong to the science club with Harry Wiggins and Wilbur Irkman?"

Mark scooted forward in his seat. "What if I was? Science is a good thing."

"Is that where you learned to build a meth lab so you could sell drugs on the street?" Derrick pressed.

Mark leaned his head on his hand. "Are you kidding? I thought this was about Natalie."

"It is." Dr. Lake steered the conversation back to the

original question. "An autopsy proved that Natalie Cummings was murdered here the night she gave birth. We've just viewed tapes of the delivery and recovery room."

Mark's odd eyes twitched sideways. "You think one of the docs killed her?"

"Why would you say that?" Derrick asked.

"I don't know." Mark shrugged. "I barely remember that night. Janie was in charge of the recovery room. We weren't very busy, so I went to help out in the nursery. They were short-staffed."

"You weren't in the recovery room when Natalie was there?"

"No, check with the neonatal unit." Mark stood. "Now if that's it, I need to finish my shift."

Brianna frowned. Something about Mark disturbed her.

He'd claimed innocence, but he could be lying. He could have easily donned surgical garb, and slipped into the recovery area unnoticed.

He had medical knowledge and could have known about Natalie's heart murmur. He'd also know exactly how to kill her without bringing attention to the crime or himself.

But if he'd killed her, why hadn't he taken Ryan that night?

Sheriff Cramer's cell phone jangled, and he stepped aside to answer the call. A second later, he snapped his phone closed. "I have to go."

"What is it?" Derrick asked.

"One of the county deputies spotted a fire in the

mountains near an abandoned cabin and shed. He says it looks like a meth lab."

Derrick jumped up, and Brianna stood. If this was the meth lab they'd been looking for, they might find answers at the site.

CRAMER LED THE WAY THROUGH THE mountain roads with his siren wailing. Night had fallen, the dark clouds obliterating the moon, the hint of more snow on the way scenting the frigid air.

Derrick drove Brianna's car, the revelations of the day weighing heavily on his mind. Twenty miles deep into the Blue Ridge Mountains, Cramer veered off onto a side road that wove through the trees and hills.

Hidden by the forest and jutting ridges, it was isolated, the perfect spot for an illegal lab.

"Look," Brianna said, pointing toward the woods ahead. "I see smoke."

He nodded. The thick plumes swirled upward through the spiny branches of the trees rising to the heavens.

Cramer screeched ahead, and Derrick shifted gears, the tires churning over the graveled road. They drove another mile, then rounded a curve and he hissed at the sight of the flames shooting from the old cabin and woodshed.

If this was their meth lab, someone had set it on fire. Someone who'd known they were onto them and wanted to get rid of the evidence.

He lurched to a stop behind Cramer, and they climbed out. Cramer was on his phone, and Derrick heard him asking for a fire engine and crime unit to be dispatched to the address.

Heat seared his face as they walked closer, and Brianna gasped. "Derrick, oh, my God, there's a baby blanket on the porch."

Panic stabbed at him, and Brianna suddenly screamed and started running forward. He grabbed her by the arm. "No, stay here."

She tried to pull away, but he jerked her to him and forced her to look at him. "Dammit, Bri, it's too dangerous. Stay here."

He released her abruptly, the sound of the crackling wood and roof collapsing echoing in the air as he ran toward the fire.

Dear God, he prayed. *Please don't let Ryan be inside. And if he is, let him be alive.*

Chapter Fifteen

Brianna's heart pounded with fear as she watched Derrick rush into the burning cabin. The woodshed beside it was completely engulfed in flames.

"What the hell is he doing?" the sheriff yelled.

"There was a baby blanket on the porch," Brianna cried.

Sheriff Cramer jerked his head toward her, his eyes widening. "He thinks Ryan might be inside?"

Brianna released a sob and nodded, then Beau ran toward the cabin, as well. Beau dashed through the front door, covering his mouth with his hand to stem the smoke.

Brianna coughed as it invaded her lungs, then closed her eyes. The thought of losing Derrick and Ryan sent an ache through her that made her nearly double over.

"Please let them be okay," she whispered. "Please, God. I'll let Derrick have Ryan and raise him. Just don't let them die."

Heat scalded her face and body as she inched closer trying to see inside. The back rooms were raging with fire, wood snapped and part of the roof caved in. Then she saw one of the men fall.

She screamed and ran forward, but her cell phone trilled, catching her off guard. Inside, she saw a man pushing himself back up—was it Derrick or Beau? The flames were spreading inside the room now, more wood splintering and falling. The window suddenly exploded and glass sprayed the ground and porch.

Her phone trilled again, and she jerked it up and stared at the caller ID. Unknown.

She started to ignore it, but a sliver of panic shot through her, and she punched the connect button.

"I warned you," a deep male voice said. "Now it's too late."

DERRICK SEARCHED THE FRONT room of the house and the kitchen, heat searing his skin as he dodged falling debris and flames. Wood popped and crackled, the flames hissing as they climbed the walls and ate the dried rotting wood. The rickety kitchen table was ablaze, the sofa smoking as fire consumed it, smoke billowing in a suffocating cloud.

"McKinney, you need to get out!" Cramer shouted.

"I have to see if the baby is in here!" Derrick shoved him aside and ran to the back rooms, but the ceiling had crashed, a wall of fire raging around him.

He started to make his way through it, but Cramer grabbed his arm. "It's too late, the back is totally engulfed."

Derrick slammed him aside, choking on the smoke and trying to find a way around the flames. Another part of the ceiling crashed down, and he jumped back to keep it from hitting him in the head. A falling beam slammed Cramer in the back, and he went down, flames eating at his shirt.

Derrick cursed, and reached for Cramer to help him up. Cramer was beating at the fire on his sleeve, and Derrick slid an arm around his waist and helped him outside.

Cramer leaned against his car, trying to catch his breath, and Derrick started back toward the house, but the entire structure exploded as if a bomb had gone off. It was the chemicals reacting, the end of the meth lab.

And maybe his son.

Brianna screamed and ran toward him, and he pulled her up against him, shielding her from the flames as the house and side building crumbled into the fire.

"No, no, no…" Brianna cried. She gripped Derrick's arms. "Was the baby inside?"

"I don't know," Derrick said in a hoarse whisper. "He wasn't in the front rooms, but I couldn't make it to the bedrooms."

She doubled over on a sob. "He was. I know he was, Derrick. The kidnapper called while you were inside."

Cold fury raced through his blood. "What? What did he say?"

Tears streamed down her ashen cheeks as she looked into his eyes. "He said he warned us…that it was too late."

She broke into hysterical sobs, and Derrick yanked her up against him and buried his head in her hair. Emotions choked his throat, his body shaking with the effort not to scream his rage and grief.

A siren suddenly wailed in the distance, and Cramer ushered him and Brianna back, away from the blaze.

"Hang in there, McKinney," Cramer said. "I'll get CSI to check for a body once the fire dies down."

Derrick glared at him. Cramer was obviously trying

to help, but the image his words painted sent Brianna even deeper into sobs, and his own eyes filled with tears.

THE NEXT TWO HOURS PASSED IN a blurry daze as the firefighters and crime unit finally arrived.

Brianna held on to Derrick, afraid if he released her, she'd drop to the ground and never be able to get up. His big body shuddered against hers, and she knew he was battling his own panic and fear.

"Brianna, shh," he said softly. "Listen to me. We can't give up hope. Ryan may not have been in that house at all."

"But the caller…he said it was too late."

Derrick punched in Ben's number. "Ben, a call from the kidnapper just came through. Did you get a trace?"

Brianna held her breath and leaned close to the phone to hear his response.

"Sorry, but the call was too short."

Derrick cursed and thanked him, then disconnected.

Tears blurred her vision and Derrick lifted her chin, his own eyes full of turmoil. "It's possible he just wanted to make us think Ryan was gone so we'd stop looking."

She latched on to that suggestion. "How could anyone be so cruel?"

His jaw tightened, then he crushed her against him and kissed her hair. "I don't know, but I'm not giving up."

His words bolstered her courage, and she swiped at her eyes. The sheriff walked over to them, his expression bleak. "McKinney, why don't you drive Brianna home? It's going to take time for the fire to completely die down and cool so the crime team can sort through the mess."

Derrick glanced back at the dwindling flames and ashes. "I should stay."

"No, you're too close," Cramer said. "Besides, there's nothing you can do here." He glanced at her. "Standing here, torturing yourself in the freezing cold won't do either of you any good."

Her lungs constricted at the thought of leaving, then she shivered as the wind picked up, ripping through her with an icy chill that bit all the way to her bone.

"The temperature is dropping again." Cramer patted Derrick's shoulder. "I'll phone you if the guys find anything."

Derrick hesitated, stroking Brianna's back as the wind shook snow from the branches like rain. "All right. As long as you keep me posted."

"I will," the sheriff vowed. "You have my word." He glanced at Brianna. "Try not to give up, Brianna."

She bit her lip, knowing he was right, but the sight of that baby blanket and the kidnapper's words were tearing her up inside.

Derrick ushered her toward the car, and she huddled in the passenger seat while he climbed behind the wheel and started the engine.

But as he drove down the mountain, she turned to look back at the burning rubble and smoke curling into the sky, and guilt assailed her.

She'd failed Ryan by not stopping the kidnapper, and now she felt as if she was abandoning him, as well.

IMAGES OF ALL THE CASES HE'D investigated taunted Derrick as he drove back to Brianna's house.

A house fire where three children had died. A car crash with an infant inside. A little boy burned when his father had punished him by throwing a pot of hot water on his face.

His own son couldn't have been in that fire. It was too horrific for him to accept.

Yet he knew the depths of evil that possessed some people, the ones lacking a soul.

He blinked away the images, reminding himself that he hadn't actually seen an infant in the cabin, and that the kidnapper could have simply wanted to make them believe the baby was dead.

If it took him until the day he died, he would find the cold son of a bitch and kill him with his bare hands.

Brianna had lapsed into a pained silence, her breathing labored. By the time they reached her house, the snow had thickened to a haze of white and the wind had intensified, whistling shrilly as they rushed inside.

He flipped on a light, and Brianna paused to look at the Christmas tree. Twinkling lights danced across the den, almost macabre in light of the empty house and desolation scenting the room. The sight of the baby stocking made his stomach clench.

Then he spotted the photographs of Ryan sitting on the side table and mantle and his heart broke.

He helped Brianna remove her coat, frowning at the way she continued to tremble, afraid she was going into shock. He rubbed her arms with his hands trying to warm her. "You're freezing," he said in a gruff voice. "I'll light a fire."

The urge to soothe and protect her overwhelmed him.

The need to have her up against him, to have her hold him and assure him, was just as strong. She looked at him as if she didn't know what to do with herself, then mumbled that she was going to take a hot shower.

He wanted to join her, but forced himself not to touch her or he'd sweep her into his arms, carry her up the steps and warm her with his body and hands. Instead, he watched her retreat, his own pain and guilt immobilizing him.

He rushed to the side porch where she kept a stack of firewood, brought it inside and lit the kindling. But the glow of the flames and the sound of the crackling wood reminded him of the meth fire, and instead of warding off the chill, it resurrected the fear that Ryan had died tonight.

That he had failed as a father.

That he hadn't been able to save his own son, the most important person in the world.

The sound of the shower kicking on echoed from above, then the muffled sound of Brianna crying. His gut twisted, and he went outside to drown out the sounds.

Filled with rage and anguish, he stepped off the porch and stared into the thick dense woods and rising mountains, then sat down on the porch steps, bowed his head and silently howled his despair into the emptiness.

BRIANNA COULDN'T STOP SHAKING.

She stripped her clothes and stepped beneath the hot water, letting the tears fall as the hot water sluiced over her.

She quickly scrubbed her body and hair, then leaned back into the water, closed her eyes and tried to banish the images of the fire.

She imagined Ryan lying in the crib, snuggled safely beneath his blanket, his teddy bear by his side. Then she saw pictures of him as he grew, as he learned to smile and coo, as he learned to walk and talk.

In her mind, she saw Derrick there picking him up, swinging him around, chasing him in the yard. The two of them hand in hand taking him to the park, pushing him on the swing, teaching him to ride a bike.

Foolish.

Even if they did find Ryan, Derrick would raise him as his own. She wouldn't be a part of their lives.

The thought choked her up again, but she swallowed back her self-pity. She hadn't indulged in that emotion when she had lived in the orphanage, and she refused to now.

The only thing that mattered was finding Ryan alive and keeping him safe from harm.

They hadn't seen him in that fire—she refused to believe he was gone. She refused to give up.

Straightening, she flipped off the water, dried off and pulled on a thick terry cloth robe. She blew dry her hair, patted her tear-swollen eyes, then forced her chin up. Sliding her feet into her slippers, she knotted the robe at her waist and left her room, pausing for only a moment to look at the empty baby bed inside the nursery. She'd wanted to paint and decorate the room, maybe with ships or animal characters, but hadn't had the chance.

Derrick would fix a room for him at his own house when he brought Ryan home.

Her resolve in place, she descended the stairs, expecting to see Derrick in front of the fire, but he wasn't inside. She checked the kitchen, but it was empty, then she walked to the front and looked out the window.

Her lungs constricted as she spotted him slumped on the front porch steps. His head was bowed, his face in his hands, his shoulders shaking. The sight wrenched something deep inside of her.

She understood his fear, pain and guilt. Derrick had been strong for her so far. She had to be strong for him now.

Even if he didn't love her, if he had loved Natalie, she loved him.

She'd known it for years, that her heart belonged to him. It always had. It always would.

Sucking in a breath for courage, she pushed open the door and stepped outside. The wind swirled her hair around her face, and she tucked it behind her ears, then inched closer to Derrick. His body was trembling with silent sobs.

So tough. So strong. So protective of others. How many children had he saved?

How many had he lost? Those probably ate at his soul and conscience just as the kids she couldn't save did her own.

She laid her hand on his shoulder, and he immediately tensed. "Go back inside, Bri."

"Not without you," she whispered.

His body went more rigid, and he swiped his hands over his face. "Please, just go."

She moved around in front of him and knelt on the steps, then pulled his hands away from his face. The anguish in his eyes and tears on his cheeks sent a streak of pain and love through her. "No."

"Please…I want to be alone." He choked on the word, but she gripped his fingers instead and pulled him up.

"No. Come inside and sit with me by the fire."

He shook his head, but she gently cupped his face in her hands, then leaned forward and pressed her lips to his jaw, his eyes, his lips.

He groaned a guttural response, then fused his mouth with hers in a fury of raw need that swept her away with its intensity.

HE THREW CANDY DOWN ON THE BED and tore off her clothes.

She kissed him feverishly. "I've been missing you, sweetheart."

"Me, too," he growled. But now that they'd gotten rid of the kid, his libido was back, and he wanted to pound himself inside his girlfriend.

"You think we're in the clear?" she asked.

"Sure as hell." He lowered his head and bit at her nipple. "We're getting so far out of town no one will ever find us."

She spread her legs, and he thrust inside her, pumping wildly as the bedsprings creaked and groaned. Candy wrapped her legs around him and bit at his neck, and they both forgot about the money and the baby as he spilled his frustration into her.

Chapter Sixteen

Derrick couldn't resist Brianna's kiss.

He'd never tasted anything so sweet, so giving, so innocent. So loving.

He didn't deserve it, but he craved her touch with every ounce of his sorry being.

She made a soft sound in her throat, and shivered. Although his mind was numb with the thrill of finally tasting her, he realized they were outside, and she was wearing only her robe. The thought of her naked skin beneath it made his body harden.

Slowly, he broke the kiss. "Let's go inside."

She nodded, and he took her hands and pulled her inside. Firelight flickered across her golden skin, the warmth cocooning them in a hazy sensual glow. Time and reality slipped away.

He had wanted Brianna when he was young, but he hadn't been good enough for her. He still wasn't.

But he needed her tonight. And he didn't have the willpower to resist.

She lifted her hand and stroked his jaw. "Derrick?"

"You should rest," he said, trying to do the right thing.

"No, I need to be with you." She traced a finger over his jaw. "And I think you need me."

God, did he....

She moved closer to him, so close he inhaled the sweet strawberry scent of body wash lingering on her skin, saw her irises darken as she lowered her eyelids, heard the hiss of her breath as she pressed her lips to his again.

The fire crackled behind them, glowing off her radiant face, and he deepened the kiss, nipping at her lips until she parted them, and he delved inside with his tongue. She threaded her fingers in his hair, and he slid his arms around her, pulling her into his embrace.

She fit perfectly.

Her breasts brushed his chest, sending an erotic thrill through him, and he slid his hand down to pull her hips against him. His hands itched to tear off that robe, his body ached, his sex throbbed.

Their tongues danced and mated, her hips moving against his, and he dragged his lips from hers, then trailed them over the soft shell of her ear and her neck. She made a low throaty sound of pleasure, and hunger ripped through him.

He lifted his head slightly and looked into her eyes. If she wanted him to stop, he had to. But the desire and heat flaming in her look stole his breath.

Emboldened, he kissed her again, this time so deeply that she moaned and clung to his arms. He swept his tongue over her throat again, then lower, pulling the edges of the robe apart to tease the curve of her breasts.

She leaned her head back in silent offering, an erotic

gesture that sent a tingle of desire through his finger-tips. Slowly he untied the belt at her waist and pulled the edges of the garment apart, revealing the most gorgeous woman he'd ever laid eyes on.

She had been pretty as a young girl, but she was beautiful now. Her skin glowed in the firelight, her breasts were heavy and full, the tips stiffening to peaks that made his groin ache. And her hips flared enticingly, the triangle of curls at the juncture of her thighs begging for his touch.

He dipped his head and traced his tongue over one turgid peak, then the other, smiling at the purr of excitement Brianna whispered into the air. Cradling her bare hips in his hand beneath the robe, he tugged one nipple into his mouth and suckled her.

"Oh, Derrick," she moaned.

He deepened the movement, wetting her with his tongue and savoring her response as she dug her hands into his hair. He laved one nipple then the other, moving his fingers over her hips, then licking his way down her flat belly until her legs buckled.

"Derrick…"

"Shh, I want you, Bri."

Her moan of pleasure echoed in the air as he lowered her to the braided rug in front of the fire and ripped off the robe so that she lay naked in front of him, a feast for his starved eyes.

BRIANNA'S ENTIRE BODY SANG with pleasure. Derrick had lowered her to the floor, and she sighed and reached for his clothes. It wasn't fair that she was naked and he was still dressed.

She wanted to see him, touch him, feel every inch of his bare flesh against hers.

She slowly unbuttoned his shirt, and he shrugged out of it, the feral look in his eyes arousing her to the point of torture. He tossed the shirt aside, then she reached for his belt buckle and yanked it free.

A small smile curved his mouth, and her hand slid lower, stroking over the hard length pressing against the fly of his jeans. He growled, then shoved her hand away, stood and shucked off his jeans.

He looked exquisite, a portrait of masculinity with thick biceps and thighs, corded muscles rippling across his abdomen, and a faint dusting of hair across his chest that tapered down and disappeared into the waistband of his boxers.

Hunger and need spiraled through her and she reached out and shoved his boxers down his legs. His sex jutted free, thick and hard, and she cupped him in her palm and stroked him.

"Brianna…" he groaned. The dark shadows in his eyes flickered with desire, and he lowered himself to the rug and took her in his arms. A frenzy of arms and legs, of tongue lashes and kisses, and touching swept her into an erotic torrent.

He licked his way down her body, suckling and kissing and nipping at her sensitive skin, using his fingers in magic ways that made her body quiver beneath his touch.

He edged her legs apart, and licked her inner thighs, then traced his damp tongue over her sensitive nub. She cried out as pleasure rocked through her.

Her moan of joy must have excited him because he spread her more open to him, and loved her the way no other man ever had. Unable to tame her desire, she bucked beneath his titillating torture and welcomed the force of his mouth tipping her over the edge.

He didn't stop then. He kissed and licked and suckled her until she finally begged him to join his body with hers. With a groan, she pulled him up her body, wrapped her legs around him and urged him to make her his.

For a brief moment, he stopped, then he reached for his jeans, yanked a condom from the pocket, ripped it open and began to roll it on. His hands were urgent and shaky, sweat beading his lip, their breathing erratic, and she reached up, took the end and rolled it over his length.

He kissed her again and pleasure obliterated the insecure voice that screamed that he didn't love her. That he'd wanted her best friend.

Instead, she closed her eyes, imagined him whispering her name in love and savored the moment their bodies became one.

DERRICK THRUST INSIDE BRIANNA, his heart racing as she opened and welcomed him. She clawed at his back, urging him deeper, and he pushed his length inside her, the taste of her pleasure still heady on his tongue.

She arched her back, and he felt her muscles clench around his, her body shuddering as another orgasm rippled through her. His own teetered on the edge, robbing his sanity, and he suckled her neck, pulsing inside her.

Mind-numbing sensations pummeled him as his

release began to strip him of reason, and he intensified the pressure of their bodies, lifting her hips until he sank himself all the way to her core.

She cried out his name, holding onto him as he hammered his way home, his body shuddering as a flood of erotic sensations and emotions overcame him. He buried his head against her chest, holding her tight.

She sighed and wrapped her arms around him, her chest rising with each labored breath. He rolled her sideways to keep from crushing her with his weight, and she curled in his embrace.

He'd finally made love with Brianna, the girl of his dreams.

But reality intruded. The sound of the fire reminded him of the earlier explosion. Of his missing son.

How could he indulge himself in such pleasure when his son might be dead?

And if he wasn't, he was missing, out there somewhere in the dark with a total stranger who might not care what happened to him at all.

He started to pull away, but Brianna clutched his arms. "Please don't go, Derrick."

Dammit. Her soft plea tore at him. He didn't want to leave her. He didn't want to be alone. He wanted her in his arms, at least for this one night.

But most of all, he wanted to pretend that he would get his son back.

BRIANNA CURLED INTO DERRICK'S arms and drifted to sleep, desperately banishing the fear that crowded her chest. She expected him to fall asleep now that they were in her bed, but he nuzzled her neck, and within minutes, they were making love again.

His hunger mounted this time, his touches gentle but eager, the desire and need even more urgent than before, as if by leaving the bed, the horrible reality would return.

The reality neither of them wanted to face.

He drove her wild with his tongue and hands, bringing her to orgasm after orgasm, and stirring emotions that she'd fought since the day she'd seen him holding those lilies for Natalie's grave.

Finally, she fell into a deep sleep, her body warm and sated, her mind filled with the memory of Derrick loving her and making her his.

But dreams shattered her euphoria. Dreams of Ryan being ripped from her arms. Of Ryan dying in the fire and never coming home.

DISTURBED BY THE TUMULTUOUS feelings bombarding him, Derrick slid from bed and tugged on his boxers, jeans and shirt. Still his breath stalled in his chest as he gazed down at Brianna's sleeping form. She moaned his name again then grabbed his pillow and pressed it to her, inhaling his scent.

He smiled, an odd twinge pulling at his chest. She was so damn beautiful. So damn loving. So damn giving.

But she'd been Natalie's best friend. And now he'd slept with them both.

A big mistake.

He had a son with Natalie, a son they still had to find.

Certain he wouldn't rest anymore, he went downstairs and stoked the fire. Anxious for news, he checked his phone but there were no messages, so once again he rummaged through the box holding Natalie's things.

First the notes about Brianna and then about the meth lab and her fear that someone was following her. He dug deeper and searched for any files concerning Ryan, of her request for Brianna to raise her son.

But there were none inside.

Frowning, he decided to search Brianna's desk. She must have removed them and filed them somewhere else. He dug through her desk, noting bills and a work calendar along with a birthday card or two from Natalie.

Then he spotted a file folder marked adoption, and opened it up. He skimmed the paperwork legally giving Brianna custody of Ryan. But Natalie's signature stopped him.

The signature…

His heart pounded, and he grabbed a card Natalie had sent to Bri that he'd seen in the desk, then compared the signatures. Anger roiled inside him as he noted the way she dotted the *I* in Natalie. It was the same small circle Brianna used when she'd signed her name on those release papers from the paramedics.

He gripped the papers with a sweaty hand, his mind racing. Brianna had forged Natalie's signature so she could gain custody of Ryan.

She'd told him that she didn't know if Ryan was his, but what if she had?

Women on previous cases had deceived their child's father to keep the man out of the baby's life.

What if Brianna wasn't the innocent sweet girl he'd believed her to be?

If she'd lied about the paperwork, and deceived him, what else had she lied about? Had she kept Ryan from him so she could have him herself?

His hands bunched into fists.

Had she seduced him tonight because she feared he'd find out?

Her soft voice called his name, then he looked up and saw her standing in the doorway.

Dammit. He was such a fool. He'd trusted the wrong woman again.

Chapter Seventeen

Brianna stared at the papers in Derrick's hands, a sick knot catching in her chest.

She knew exactly what Derrick had found—the papers she'd fudged so there wouldn't be any question as to her request for custody being approved.

She could lose her job, possibly even go to jail.

But the look in Derrick's eyes was even worse.

"Natalie never signed Ryan over to you."

Disappointment, accusations and contempt edged his gruff voice. "You knew all along that Ryan was mine, but instead of contacting me, you forged papers so you could adopt him." He waved the papers in the air. "It's true, isn't it? You lied to me. You knew but you wanted Ryan, and the only reason I found out about him was because he was kidnapped."

She shook her head, hating the hurt on his face. "No, Derrick…."

"Don't lie now, Brianna," Derrick said coldly. "I can see for myself that you signed Natalie's name here. Any expert certainly could." He stalked toward her. "But you had it all covered, didn't you. With your job, you just pushed things through, so no one asked questions."

Brianna released a shaky breath, and clutched her robe around her, glad she'd slipped it on. "That part is true," she whispered, her voice choking. "But it's not like you think, Derrick. I swear I didn't know you were the father, Natalie lied to me about that."

"Why would she lie? You were her best friend."

Because she'd known that Bri was in love with Derrick. That she'd wanted him all her life.

But she couldn't say those words now. He'd never believe her.

"Why? Because you didn't think I was fit to be a father?"

The pain in those words wrenched her heart. "No, Derrick, you've got it all wrong. That's not the reason at all, I swear I didn't know the truth." She reached for him, but he jerked away.

"Don't touch me, Bri. That sweet little seductive act won't work anymore."

"Derrick, you have to listen to me," she said, barely able to breathe. "Natalie was panicked and afraid that night when she went into labor just like I said. And she did make me promise to take care of Ryan. I swear that's true, and then she died, and everything fell apart. I was grieving and in shock, and I was afraid that if I didn't get custody of Ryan that he'd go in the system and—"

"Stop it!" Derrick shouted. "I don't want to hear any more of your lies."

The look of contempt in his eyes sent a sharp pain through her chest. She reached for him again. Only an hour earlier, they'd been curled up in bed together. They'd made love over and over. He had to know how she felt.

"Please," she whispered. "I love you, Derrick."

"I can't believe I actually trusted you," he hissed. "That I fell for your act. You're just like the rest of the women I've known. You'll lie and sleep with anyone to get what you want."

"No…." Pain stabbed her heart. "I love you, Derrick. I always have. That's why Natalie didn't tell me you were Ryan's father."

"I said to stop with the lies." He grabbed his socks and shoes and stuffed them on, then his coat and stalked toward the door, his movements jerky and filled with rage as he yanked open the door. With a snarl, he pivoted and gave her an icy look. "I'm going to find my son, and when I do, Brianna, I will get custody of him, and I never want to see you again."

The winter wind whistled through the house as he left, but the painful chill inside her had nothing to do with the cold.

Even if he found Ryan, she'd lost them both.

DERRICK STORMED FROM THE house, frustration and anguish clawing at him. He wanted to pound out his anger into something—into someone.

How had he let Brianna get under his skin?

He jumped in her car, and tore down the mountain, self-recriminations screaming in his head. Yet even as he told himself that Brianna had used him, had seduced him, the sight of her tears as he'd left, of her begging him to listen, made his chest clench.

Brianna had never been deceitful, not in school. She'd always been loving and kind and helped bring families together. She had loved Natalie beyond belief.

And hadn't Natalie written that she didn't want to tell Bri about his night with her because Bri had always crushed on him?

Dammit. He didn't know what to believe.

Maybe he'd overreacted to those papers because he was so afraid he'd lost his son. Because if Natalie had trusted him, she would have told him about the pregnancy. Maybe Bri truly had only been trying to protect Ryan.

And last night when he'd been so distraught, she'd given herself to him.

Bri had never slept around.

He started to spin the car around and go back to her and have it out, but his phone buzzed, and he checked the number. Sheriff Cramer.

God, what if he had bad news?

Inhaling sharply, he quickly stabbed the connect button. "McKinney."

"Derrick, it's Cramer."

A tense second passed. "Yeah?"

"The rescue workers didn't find a body in the fire."

Relief surged through him, making it difficult to swallow much less breathe. "No baby?"

"No. No one." Cramer coughed. "I have more news. We found a print at the house."

Hope exploded in his chest. "Whom did it belong to?"

"A kid named Jeremy Dahl. He was arrested for a possession charge last year, but his lawyer got him off."

"I talked to him," Derrick said. "But he denied knowing anything about the lab."

"He lied. We need to talk to him again."

Adrenaline surged through Derrick. "I'll meet you at his house."

Cramer gave him the address, and he steered the car toward town. Ten minutes later, he met Cramer at the Dahls' house, a sprawling Georgian structure on three acres in a new development that catered to the wealthier sect of Sanctuary. Bright red bows and wreaths adorned the windows, a tree had been lit up outside and through the window he spotted another one in the dining area that touched the twenty-foot ceiling.

Cramer scrubbed his hand over his beard stubble, and Derrick realized the man had been at the scene of the fire all night and hadn't slept. Derrick rang the doorbell and the sound chimed through the house.

A maid answered and escorted them in. Derrick noted the expensive furnishings, a collection of carolers in a glass case, and miniature crystal snowmen lining the mantle of the great room.

This kid probably had everything he'd ever wanted— but he'd turned to drugs.

A middle-aged man in a pricey-looking business suit appeared and glanced between them with a scowl. "Sheriff Cramer?"

"Hello, Mr. Dahl." He introduced Derrick, then asked to talk to his son.

"What is this about?" Mr. Dahl asked.

"Just get your son and we'll explain."

"Perhaps I should call my lawyer first?" Dahl suggested.

Cramer crossed his arms. "That's up to you, Mr. Dahl. We're simply here to ask questions, not make an arrest. But if you'd rather do this down at the station..."

"No. I'll get him." Mr. Dahl disappeared for a moment, then returned. Jeremy was dressed in jeans and a football jersey, a surly attitude on his face.

He cut his eyes toward Cramer, then Derrick, and jammed his hands in the pockets of his faded jeans. "I need to leave for school."

"This won't take long," Cramer said.

Mr. Dahl gestured for them to sit down and Jeremy slumped on the leather sofa, twisting his hands in his lap.

Cramer disclosed facts about the meth lab they'd discovered and the fire.

Dahl stood abruptly. "My son is not involved in drugs."

Jeremy bit his lip but stared at his hands.

"Mr. Dahl," Cramer interjected. "We know that Jeremy was arrested for possession and your lawyer made the charges disappear."

"So?" Jeremy muttered. "That was last year."

Jeremy's father gave him a warning look.

"What do you know about this meth lab?" Cramer asked.

"Nothing," Jeremy answered.

Derrick's temper rose. "That's what you said at the school. But if that's true, why were your fingerprints found at the site where the lab burned down?"

Panic lit Jeremy's eyes, and his father cursed.

"Jeremy?" his father said sternly. "I thought you said you were clean now."

"I am," Jeremy stuttered. "I just went there with a friend."

"What friend?" Cramer asked.

"Just a friend," Jeremy exclaimed. "But we didn't burn the place down."

"Jeremy was at home last night," his father insisted. "I picked him up after practice and we came straight here."

"Look, Mr. Dahl," Derrick cut in. "I don't really give a crap about the drugs or the lab, but this may have something to do with my son being kidnapped and the murder of Natalie Cummings, the baby's mother."

"What?" Dahl narrowed his eyes. "What's a meth lab got to do with a kidnapping and murder?"

Derrick explained their theory.

"I didn't have anything to do with Ms. Cummings's death or that kid being stolen," Jeremy bellowed.

His father stood and reached for the phone.

"Dad, I swear I didn't," Jeremy muttered. "I admit to going to the meth lab, and yeah, I even tried a hit but that was it. I don't know anything about this other stuff."

"What about a group called The Club?" Derrick asked. "We think they burned down the hospital years ago during an accidental explosion. Are they responsible for this lab?"

Jeremy shifted sideways. "Like I said, I don't know nothing about the kidnapping or murder."

"Jeremy," his father called through gritted teeth. "Tell them what you do know. Who started the lab?"

Jeremy glared at his father, but Mr. Dahl gave him a stern look and Jeremy grunted. "Some old guy started it."

"What old guy?" Derrick asked.

"A drug salesman, you know, a legitimate one."

"You mean a pharmaceutical salesman?"

Jeremy shrugged. "He contacted a couple of the science geeks and they built the lab. Name's Irkel or something like that."

"Irkman," Derrick suggested. "Wilbur Irkman." He glanced at Cramer. "I heard his name from someone else."

"There, he's told you what he knows," Mr. Dahl said. "Now you'll leave him out of this, won't you, Sheriff?"

Cramer stood, hands on his hips. "As long as he's telling the truth."

Derrick gave him a cold look. "And if you lied, Jeremy, jail will be the least of your problems."

BRIANNA PACED IN FRONT OF THE fireplace, haunted by the sight of Derrick walking out. Where was he now? Was he looking for Ryan?

Would he come back? Would he even let her know when he had found the baby?

She slumped onto the sofa then dropped her head forward into her hands. God, she'd made such a mess of things. First she'd lost Ryan.

And now she'd lost Derrick, the only man she'd ever loved.

Too agitated to sit still, she jumped up and paced across the room, pausing to study the photos of Ryan again.

She could survive if Derrick didn't love her, but they had to find his son.

She had to do something; she just couldn't sit here and wait.

Adrenaline kicking in, she grabbed a pad of paper and listed all the people they'd questioned.

First the two couples, the Phillipses and Hamptons. Principal Billings. Ace Atkins. Jeremy Dahl. Evan Rutherford. Wilbur Irkman.

Then the hospital staff—Dr. Thorpe. And Mark Larimer.

Dr. Thorpe seemed sincere, but something about Mark had made her feel uncomfortable.

Hadn't his name been mentioned in relation to the science club years ago?

She glanced at the box holding Natalie's things, remembered the yearbooks inside, dug out the one from eight years ago and flipped through it.

She found the photograph of the science club and studied Wilbur Irkman's picture, then Mark's. She recognized a few of the others, but most of them had moved away.

Wilbur had been out of town when they'd gone to his house.

And Mark worked at the hospital. He could have easily slipped into the recovery room and no one would have noticed. And with his medical knowledge, he'd know just how to kill.

She rushed up the steps to dress. She had to make Mark tell her the truth. She threw on jeans and a sweater, socks and boots then ran down the steps to grab her keys. Then she remembered that Derrick had taken her car.

She punched in the number for Sanctuary's taxi service, then phoned the hospital to see if Mark was on duty. Thankfully he was working the morning shift.

Twenty minutes later, the cab driver dropped her off at the hospital. She shivered as she jogged up the steps and rushed inside, but determination spurned her on. Even if she couldn't have Ryan and Derrick, she could help bring Derrick's son home.

She rode the elevator to the labor and delivery floor, then asked for Mark at the nurse's desk. "He's with a patient, but I'll tell him you're here."

She nodded, glancing at the nursery as she waited. Even though she hadn't given birth to Ryan, she'd loved that baby with all her heart. He was a part of her best friend and the man she loved—how could she not love their child?

The nurses and volunteers were bustling around, the food carts delivering breakfast clinking on the linoleum floor. Suddenly she felt something sharp jab at her back.

"Miss Honeycutt?"

She stiffened at the sound of Mark's low cold voice.

"There's a gun at your back," he growled. "Scream or make a move and I'll shoot."

Chapter Eighteen

Derrick followed Cramer in his squad car to Wilbur Irkman's residence, his pulse racing. Maybe they were finally going to get some answers.

He'd beat them out of the man if he had to.

Ryan had been missing too damn long.

Cramer had agreed to keep his siren off so as not to alarm Irkman in case he heard them and decided to run. Dahl had promised that his son would not contact the man and warn him they were coming, but he didn't trust anyone now. Especially a man trying to protect his son.

Ironic that his old man had beat him half to death, when this man was willing to put his money and reputation on the line to protect him and the kid was screwing up.

When he found Ryan, he would be a better father than his own. He would spend time with his boy, take him fishing and boating, teach him to ride a bike, throw a softball.

None of which his old man had done.

Would that be enough?

Ryan's mother was dead. The only person he'd bonded with was Brianna.

A fresh pain seized him. She did love Ryan. But had she lied when she said she'd loved him?

Could he ever trust her again?

Cramer screeched to a stop at the Irkman house, and Derrick stopped and threw Brianna's car into Park. Gritting his teeth against the chill, he and Cramer strode up to the door and Derrick pounded on it.

Wilbur's mother grumbled from the inside. "Who's there?"

"It's Sheriff Cramer," Cramer said. "Open up, ma'am."

The door screeched open, the scent of coffee and sausage filling the air, along with the scent of cigarette smoke. Mrs. Irkman flipped the cigarette up with a dismissive scowl. "What you want?"

"To see Wilbur," Cramer said.

Derrick shouldered his way past her, and walked through the rundown place, when a thin wiry man emerged from the bathroom wearing a pristine white collared shirt and dress pants. Derrick vaguely remembered the geek from high school, the guy who'd been on the Dean's List and won all the science fairs.

"What the hell?"

Derrick grabbed him by the collar and shoved him up against the wall. "We know you were involved in the meth lab that burned down last night. You also were responsible for the one eight years ago, the one that killed all those people, including women and kids."

Irkman's face totally blanched, and his eye twitched. "You can't come in here and accuse me of this."

Mrs. Irkman shrieked and pressed a hand to her chest. Cramer helped her to sit down, and gave Derrick a warning glare.

Derrick didn't care. They'd wasted enough time.

"Tell us the truth, Irkman," Derrick growled between clenched teeth. "We know you're involved, that you ran the drug operation, and that you may have wanted to cover it up just as you covered up your lab eight years ago when all those citizens of Sanctuary died. Did you have Natalie Cummings killed to protect your side business?"

Irkman began to shake. "I want a deal."

"A deal?" Derrick wanted to kill him. "Tell us the truth and maybe you won't wind up on death row."

"No…." Mrs. Irkman cried. "Wilbur, please, son, tell them you didn't kill anyone."

"He was involved in the meth lab," Cramer said to her. "He belonged to a club. The explosion that night might have been an accident but they killed dozens and dozens of innocent people and should have come forward and owned up to it."

"Not only did you get away with it," Derrick said, "but now you've started a new drug ring and are taking advantage of the kids in town."

"No, Wilbur, tell them it's not true," Mrs. Irkman screeched.

"Shut up, Mother!" Wilbur screamed. "Just shut up."

Mrs. Irkman burst into tears, and Derrick slid his hands around Wilbur's throat. "Who took my son, Irkman?"

"It wasn't me," Wilbur pleaded. "I helped set up the meth lab but that's all. I swear."

Derrick shoved his face into the scrawny man. "Then who stole my baby?"

"I don't know." Wilbur shuddered, then tried to tear Derrick's hands from around his throat.

"Who?" Derrick repeated.

"Mark Larimer," Wilburn muttered. "He and I set up the lab together but then Natalie got wind of it and figured things out."

Cramer moved closer. "Then what happened?"

"Mark paid his brother to threaten her. We thought if she was scared she wouldn't talk and we'd all be safe."

Fury ripped through Derrick. That was the reason she hadn't told Brianna or him. She'd been trying to protect Brianna and her son.

But doing so had cost her her life.

Derrick's heart pounded. "Larimer burned down the lab?"

"Yes."

"And he kidnapped Ryan?"

"He hired his brother to," Wilbur said in a shrill voice. "But he wouldn't have done that if that nosy social worker hadn't started asking questions about Natalie's death. If you want someone to blame, blame her."

Derrick wanted to choke the man, but Cramer touched his arm, his handcuffs jangling from his hand. "Don't do it, McKinney. I know you hate him now, but he and Larimer need to face the town and pay for all the people's lives they destroyed eight years ago."

Derrick trembled with the effort to release Irkman

into Cramer's hands. But Cramer was right. They should have to face the town.

And he needed to find Larimer and make him tell him where his brother had taken his son.

"WHY ARE YOU DOING THIS?" Brianna whispered as Mark dragged her outside, shoved her into the driver's seat of his car and ordered her to drive to her house.

"Because you're going to ruin everything," Mark bellowed. "You and that bitch Natalie. Why couldn't you just leave it alone? We would never have kidnapped that damn kid if you hadn't gotten so nosy."

Brianna's blood ran cold, but he shoved the gun against her temple and she started the engine and headed out of the parking lot. "Where's Ryan, Mark? What did you do with him? Is he all right?"

"I don't know where he is," Mark muttered. "But you'll never see him again."

"Mark," Brianna whispered. "Please, if you haven't hurt Ryan, we can work something out. Just take me to him and I promise not to press charges."

"It's too late for that," Mark yelled. "Too late. Just drive."

Brianna heard the panic in his voice, and forced herself to calm down. Maybe when they reached her house, she could talk some sense into him, play on his conscience.

But he had killed Natalie. And if he'd killed all those people years ago, he has nothing to lose.

Stall, she had to stall. Get home. Maybe Derrick would be waiting.

A sob of terror and hopelessness welled in her chest.

No, Derrick wouldn't come back. He'd told her that he never wanted to see her again.

She glanced at the trees lining the road and considered ramming into them. It might kill her and Mark though, and then Derrick couldn't question Mark and make him confess where his brother had taken Ryan. She vaguely remembered that Mark had a sibling. He'd been younger, a troubled guy, not very smart. How far would he go for Mark?

"Don't even think about it," Mark growled as if he'd read her mind. "You try to kill me, I'll make sure your boyfriend dies and that the kid does, too."

"Then Ryan is still alive?" she said in a low whisper.

Mark waved the gun. "Just shut up and drive."

She bit her lip to keep from crying, then turned the car toward the mountain road to her house. The seconds ticked by excruciatingly slow, but they finally arrived.

Hope died as she realized Derrick hadn't returned, that she was on her own.

Mark jumped from the car like a wild man, ran to her side, yanked her out and dragged her up the steps. She fumbled with the keys trying to stall. Contemplating whether to try to escape. If he killed her, at least Derrick might find him and make him talk.

She glanced at the woods, ready to run, but he rammed the gun in her side, and Ryan's face flashed in her mind. She wasn't ready to die.

He pushed her in the door, then hauled her across the room to the desk in her den, and forced her to sit down. Cursing beneath his breath, he scrambled for paper in the desk, shoved a piece in front of her, then grabbed a pen and jammed it into her hand.

"Start writing."

She heaved a breath, her heart roaring in her ears at the wild panic in his beady eyes. "Write what?"

"Your suicide note," he said with an evil smile. "How you killed Natalie because you wanted her baby so badly, then you couldn't handle the guilt so you abandoned him and cried kidnapping."

He leaned forward, his rancid breath bathing her face. "How you couldn't live with the guilt any longer so you had to take your own life."

CRAMER HANDCUFFED IRKMAN AND shoved him into the squad car while Derrick called the hospital to see if Larimer was on duty.

"I'm sorry, Mr. McKinney, he was here," the nurse said. "But I saw him leaving with Miss Honeycutt a few minutes ago."

Derrick clenched the phone with a white-knuckled grip. "Where was he going?"

"He didn't say," she said. "But it's not like Mark to leave during his shift. And when I tried to call out to him, he just glared at me and hurried off."

"I need his home address," Derrick said.

"Sir, I can't give out that information."

"This is a matter of life and death. The sheriff is here with me. Do you need to speak to him?"

"Well, no, I guess not." She tapped a few keys on the computer, then gave him the address.

"What's going on?" Cramer asked when Derrick ended the call.

"Larimer has Brianna."

"Damn." Cramer slammed the door shut, locking Irkman inside the back of the squad car.

Derrick punched in Brianna's number, praying she'd answer, but the phone rang and rang and no one answered.

"Put out an APB on him, and go to Larimer's," Derrick said on a curse. "I'll check Brianna's just in case he took her there."

Cramer gave a clipped nod, climbed into his car, flipped on the siren and sped away while Derrick rushed toward Brianna's. He punched her number again, his heart racing as he sped around traffic.

Brianna had to be all right. He couldn't be too late.

But he'd been too late on his last case. He'd been too late for Natalie. And maybe Ryan...

No, he wouldn't give up.

Emotions threatened to paralyze him as he turned off the road from town onto the narrow one that led to Brianna's. Gravel and snow spewed from the tires as he ground his way up the hill, but he slowed as he approached Brianna's house and parked in a clearing down from the drive. If Larimer had Brianna, he needed the element of surprise on his side.

He checked his gun, then eased open the door, climbed out and inched his way up the drive.

Fear slammed into him again when he spotted the blue truck parked near her house. He crept up the steps to the porch, then looked inside the front window. The house was dark, shadows dancing along the interior.

He paused to listen, but only the wind howling and the hiss of limbs breaking beneath the weight of the snow echoed in the silence. That and his thundering heart.

Clenching his jaw, he slipped down the steps, then around to the side window where he could see inside the den.

Fear seized him when he spotted Brianna and Larimer. Brianna was sitting at the desk in the corner. Larimer towered over her with a gun pressed to her temple. Then he shoved something into her mouth—a pill, Derrick realized when he spotted the bottle on the desk.

Larimer cocked the gun, then shoved another one in her mouth and ordered her to swallow.

BRIANNA TRIED TO SPIT OUT THE sleeping pill, but Larimer slapped her and jammed another one in her mouth. She'd tried to stall, hold them in her mouth, praying someone would come to her rescue. But she was already starting to feel the effects, starting to feel groggy.

The room was spinning, her ears ringing and the hazy blur of his face swam in front of her.

"You can kill me," she spoke through a cotton mouth, "but Derrick will find you and he'll get Ryan back."

He shook out another pill, grabbed her jaw and jammed it in her mouth. She choked and coughed, but he pressed the gun to her temple and she closed her eyes and forced herself to swallow. But her mouth was so dry, the pill stuck in her throat and she began to cough.

The floor squeaked in the kitchen, but she assumed it was the wind. Or maybe it was just her ears ringing from the drugs.

But suddenly a shout rent the air and through the fog of her mind, she saw Derrick tear Mark away from her and throw him to the floor.

A gunshot fired, and she struggled to see what was happening, but the room swam again and she slid from the chair to the floor. Another shot pinged through the air and the sound of a man grunting echoed through the room.

God, no....

Had Mark killed Derrick?

Chapter Nineteen

Derrick had lost his gun when he and Larimer had fallen, but then he slammed his fist into the side of Larimer's face. Larimer cursed and fought him, one hand still gripping his weapon, and they rolled across the floor.

With a hard whack of his hand, he knocked the gun from Larimer's hand. The gun fired again, hit the ceiling, and Larimer cursed and tried to scramble away to retrieve the weapon.

But Derrick grabbed him by the collar and slammed his fist against his face. Fury rose as he saw Brianna collapse to the floor. He straddled Larimer, then gripped him around the neck, choking him.

Larimer sputtered and coughed, and Derrick tightened his hold. "You killed Natalie, didn't you?"

Larimer's eyes widened as he struggled to breathe. He tried to pry Derrick's hands from his throat, but Derrick pressed his body down with his weight, and sank his fingers deeper into the man's fleshy neck. Then he whipped his phone from his pocket and called 9-1-1.

"What did you give her?" he asked through gritted teeth.

"Sleeping pills," Larimer hissed. "Just sleeping pills."

But too many could kill her.

"9-1-1," the operator said.

"Get an ambulance out to Brianna Honeycutt's house. She may have overdosed on sleeping pills. And call Sheriff Cramer and tell him to send a car out to the house to make an arrest." He gave her the address, and slammed the phone shut, then shook Larimer.

"You killed Natalie, didn't you?"

Larimer nodded, terror in his eyes.

"Where's the baby?"

"I don't know," Larimer screeched.

"Don't lie to me," Derrick growled. "Where is he?"

Larimer looked panicked and again tried to escape, but Derrick choked him harder. "Tell me, dammit!"

"My brother took him, but I don't know where they are…I swear I don't."

Derrick released one hand just enough to lean sideways and grab the gun. Then he shoved it in Larimer's face. "Tell me or I'm going to shoot one knee out. Then another. Then I'll work my way up." He traced the gun over the side of the man's head.

Larimer coughed and cried out, then bucked his legs and fought him for the gun. The gun went off, and suddenly Larimer's groan of pain filled the air. The bullet had hit him in the chest. Blood began to gush.

Derrick cursed. "No, you can't die, you bastard, not until you tell me where my son is!"

But Larimer sputtered and gurgled blood. It spewed

from his chest wound, then his nose and mouth. Derrick shook him. "No, dammit, you can't die. Where's my son?"

Larimer's eyes grew wide again, filled with panic and horror. Then suddenly they rolled back in his head and went blank.

Derrick choked on his own emotions. With Larimer gone, Ryan might be lost forever.

Tears blurred his vision as he rushed to Brianna and knelt to check her pulse. She couldn't be dead already. He couldn't lose her….

It took him a minute, but finally he found a pulse. It was slow and thready, but at least she was alive.

Thank God. He pulled her in his arms and held her to him, rocking her back and forth and watching her breathe as he waited on the ambulance.

BRIANNA HAD NO IDEA HOW LONG she'd been asleep, but she felt exhausted and her stomach ached. She opened her eyes and searched the dimly lit room. A white room.

The hospital.

The memory of awakening in the E.R., of having her stomach pumped, returned and she groaned.

"How are you feeling?"

She blinked, confused, then Derrick's handsome face appeared in front of her. He looked angry and worried and…as if something terrible was wrong.

"Ryan?" she whispered. Dear God, did he have bad news about the baby?

"We still don't know," he said. "Larimer said he hired his brother to kidnap him, but he didn't know where he took Ryan. Did he tell you?"

She shook her head, tears filling her eyes.

"Shh." He brushed the hair from her forehead. "Cramer has an APB out on him now, and the FBI is also looking. GAI is trying to trace that call he made to you."

She nodded, although disappointment ballooned in her chest. Nausea ripped through her, and the room swirled. She closed her eyes again, but another memory returned. Derrick walking out the door. Derrick hated her. He'd said he never wanted to see her again.

Then why was he here?

"Brianna," he said in a gruff tone. "You didn't answer me. How do you feel?"

Lost and alone and desperate to know that the baby was safe.

"Miserable," she whispered. "All this and we still don't have Ryan."

"I'll find him, I swear I will," he promised softly. "Tell me what happened. Why did you go to the hospital?"

"I decided that Mark was suspicious." She licked her dry lips. "I wanted to make him tell me where Ryan was. I wanted to bring him back to you...."

In spite of her bravado, a tear slipped down her cheek. Derrick brushed it away with his thumb. "You almost got killed trying to save my son. Even after the things I said to you?"

He sounded confused, troubled, angry. "I had to," she whispered. "I was supposed to protect Ryan and I didn't." A sob escaped her. "And I let you down. I never meant to do that, to lie to you, Derrick."

"I know," he said gently.

"What?" She blinked back more tears at the forgiveness in his voice.

His eyes darkened as they skated over her. "Did you mean everything you said?"

Emotions welled in her chest. "That I love you?" She gave a self-deprecating laugh. "Yes. But I know you loved Natalie, Derrick. I don't expect anything in return. I just wanted to bring Ryan home and give him back to you. To put him in your arms where he belongs."

An odd expression flashed in Derrick's eyes, then he dragged a chair over beside the bed, put her hand in his and leaned his head against their joined hands.

"Derrick?" Using her free hand, she brushed his hair back from his forehead. "Derrick, you're going to make a wonderful father. I promise to fix things with the court, even if I have to resign from my job. I want you to have your son and tell him all about his mother and how much you loved her."

Derrick shook his head, unable to believe Brianna's confession. Her selflessness.

Finally he swallowed, then placed a kiss on her palm.

Her eyes lifted to his, surprised and confused.

"*You* have it all wrong now," he said, the words tumbling from him. "I never loved Natalie, Bri. What happened between us was a…mistake." He cleared his throat. "I'm not proud of it. I'm sorry if that night hurt you, but I can't be completely sorry because Ryan came out of it. But I never loved Natalie."

"I don't understand…."

"I never loved her, Bri," he said, then lifted her chin with his hand. "Brianna, I love you."

"What?"

"I have always wanted you." His chest tightened at the admission. "Even in high school, but I thought you were too good for me."

"Too good for you?" she said in a low voice.

He nodded. "I told you my father beat me all the time. He told me I was worthless and I believed him. That's why I got into trouble." He hesitated. "But you were different. Even though your mother abandoned you in that orphanage, you were kind and caring and…so damn beautiful. I didn't think I deserved someone like you."

She started to speak, but he pressed a finger to her lips to silence her. He had to finish. Even after he'd hurt her, she'd risked her life for him and his son. "I thought that I wasn't father material because of my old man, and I figured you and Natalie saw me that way."

"Derrick, oh, Derrick, that's not true. I told you before. You're going to make a wonderful father."

His chest swelled, and he leaned forward and cupped her face in his hands. "I hope so," he said. "But we have to find Ryan first."

Tears blurred her eyes again, but then he lowered his mouth and kissed her. "I love you, Bri. And when we bring Ryan home, I want all of us to be a family." His voice broke. "But even without Ryan, I want to be with you."

Brianna kissed him with all the pent up love she possessed. She wanted that more than anything. Now all they had to do was find Ryan and they would be a family.

Until then, they'd love one another and keep searching for the baby who had brought them together.

Chapter Twenty

One week later

Derrick rose from Brianna's bed, filled with love for her. Yet a part of him was still empty, that throbbing part of his heart that missed his son.

Cramer had called the Feds in to bust the meth lab members. Four kids from the high school were involved, and the town rocked with the news that three hometown boys—Wilbur Irkman, Mark Larimer and Principal Billings—had been responsible for the hospital explosion years ago. Charges were being filed and the men were in jail.

He and Brianna had also filmed a television interview pleading for information about Ryan.

The FBI and GAI were still searching for Mark's brother.

Derrick's cell phone buzzed, and he glanced at the number. GAI.

Hope warred with fear as he connected the call. "McKinney."

"It's Running Deer. We have news. I tracked Mark's brother and girlfriend. The authorities have them in custody."

"What about Ryan?" Derrick held his breath.

"They claim they dropped him at an orphanage in north Georgia. I spoke with the social worker there, and she saw your plea on TV. She believes the baby is Ryan. Ben faxed over his photo and DNA and they're running tests now."

Hope fed his adrenaline. "Where is the orphanage?"

His friend gave him the address, and Derrick scribbled it down.

"Thanks. I'm on my way." Derrick disconnected the call, then raced to the bedroom. Brianna opened her eyes as he leaned over her and kissed her.

"Wake up, sleepyhead. We have a lead on Ryan."

Brianna's eyes popped open, pure joy flickering in her eyes. "Oh, Derrick, they found him?"

"A social worker found a baby dropped off at an orphanage in north Georgia." He tugged her out of bed. "They're comparing DNA now, but the social worker recognized his photograph."

Brianna shrieked with excitement, threw off her gown, ran to the dresser and began to pull out underwear. She was so beautiful. Thank God, he had a lifetime to look at her and love her.

But now they had to see their son.

They hurriedly dressed, grabbed coffee and doughnuts at a drive-thru, then settled back for the long ride to north Georgia.

It seemed to take them years to make the trip, but hope filled the car, the anticipation making them practically giddy.

Finally they reached the orphanage, and the sun slid through the clouds shining down on them as they raced up to the door. A young brunette named Simone greeted them and showed them inside.

Derrick introduced them both, and Simone smiled. "Yes, I saw you two on the news."

Derrick's chest constricted. They'd gotten their hopes up, but what if this wasn't Ryan?

"The baby's in here." Simone led them in to a cozy den. The sound of children singing echoed from another room, and he spotted a small cradle near the fire. Christmas decorations adorned the house, the twinkling lights dancing across the room.

Brianna inhaled next to him, and he took her hand and together they walked over to the cradle. His heart pounded as Simone lifted the baby and angled him so they could see his face.

Brianna gasped. "It's him. Oh, my God, Derrick, it's really Ryan."

Simone's face beamed. "The local sheriff just phoned. The DNA was a match." She gestured toward Derrick. "Would you like to hold your son, Mr. McKinney?"

Nerves knotted Derrick's neck. He'd wanted this for so long. But what if he did something wrong?

Brianna lifted her hand and stroked his back. "Go ahead, Derrick. Your son needs you."

"He needs us," Derrick said gruffly. His chest clenched as he took his baby in his arms and cradled him close.

One look in Ryan's eyes and he knew this boy was his, that he'd do anything to protect him.

Brianna lowered a kiss to Ryan's cheek, and Derrick pulled her into his embrace, holding them both against him.

He'd never liked the holidays before, especially Christmas. But this year everything had changed. Christmas had brought him a woman he loved, and a son.

Ryan cooed up at him, and Derrick grinned foolishly, silently vowing to love his new family forever.

* * * * *

Don't miss Rita Herron's next book
of romantic suspense when
RAWHIDE RANGER goes on sale
in March 2010 as part of
THE SILVER STAR OF TEXAS:
COMMANCHE CREEK.
Look for it only from Harlequin Intrigue!

'THIS EVENING I'm flying to New York for two weeks,' Jasim imparted with a casualness that made her heart sink like a stone. 'That's why I had you brought here. I own this apartment and you'll be comfortable here while I'm abroad.'

'I can afford my own accommodation although I may not need it for long. I'll have another job by the time you get back—'

Jasim released a slightly harsh laugh. 'There's no need for you to look for another position. How would I ever see you? Don't you understand what I'm offering you?'

Elinor stood very still. 'No, I must be incredibly thick because I haven't quite worked out yet what you're offering me....'

His charismatic smile slashed his lean dark visage. 'Naturally, I want to take care of you....'

'No, thanks.' Elinor forced a smile and mentally willed him not to demean her with some sordid proposition. 'The only man who will ever take *care* of me with my agreement will be my husband. I'm willing to wait for you to come back but I'm not willing to be kept by you. I'm a very independent woman and what I give, I give freely.'

Jasim frowned. 'You make it all sound so serious.'

'What happened between us last night left pure chaos in its wake. Right now, I don't know whether I'm on my head or my heels. I'll stay for a while because I have nowhere else to go in the short term. So maybe it's good that you'll be away for a while.'

Jasim pulled out his wallet to extract a card. 'My private number,' he told her, presenting her with it as though it was a precious gift, which indeed it was. Many women would have done just about anything to gain access to that direct hotline to him, but his staff guarded his privacy with scrupulous care.

Before he could close the wallet, his blood ran cold in his veins. How could he have made such a serious oversight? What if he had got her pregnant? He knew that an unplanned pregnancy would engulf his life like an avalanche, crush his freedom and suffocate him. He barely stilled a shudder at the threat of such an outcome and thought how ironic it was that what his older brother had longed and prayed for to secure the line to the throne should strike Jasim as an absolute disaster....

* * *

What will proud Prince Jasim do if Elinor is expecting his royal baby? Perhaps an arranged marriage is the only solution! But will Elinor agree? Find out in DESERT PRINCE, BRIDE OF INNOCENCE by Lynne Graham [#2884], available from Harlequin Presents® in January 2010.

Bestselling Harlequin Presents author

Lynne Graham

brings you an exciting new miniseries:

PREGNANT BRIDES

Inexperienced and expecting, they're forced to marry

Collect them all:

DESERT PRINCE, BRIDE OF INNOCENCE

January 2010

RUTHLESS MAGNATE, CONVENIENT WIFE

February 2010

GREEK TYCOON, INEXPERIENCED MISTRESS

March 2010

REQUEST YOUR FREE BOOKS!

2 FREE NOVELS
PLUS 2
FREE GIFTS!

◆ HARLEQUIN®
INTRIGUE®

Breathtaking Romantic Suspense

YES! Please send me 2 FREE Harlequin Intrigue® novels and my 2 FREE gifts (gifts are worth about $10). After receiving them, if I don't wish to receive any more books, I can return the shipping statement marked "cancel." If I don't cancel, I will receive 6 brand-new novels every month and be billed just $4.24 per book in the U.S. or $4.99 per book in Canada. That's a savings of close to 15% off the cover price! It's quite a bargain! Shipping and handling is just 50¢ per book.* I understand that accepting the 2 free books and gifts places me under no obligation to buy anything. I can always return a shipment and cancel at any time. Even if I never buy another book from Harlequin, the two free books and gifts are mine to keep forever.

182 HDN EYTR 382 HDN EYT3

Name	(PLEASE PRINT)
Address	Apt. #
City	State/Prov.	Zip/Postal Code

Signature (if under 18, a parent or guardian must sign)

Mail to the Harlequin Reader Service:
IN U.S.A.: P.O. Box 1867, Buffalo, NY 14240-1867
IN CANADA: P.O. Box 609, Fort Erie, Ontario L2A 5X3

Not valid to current subscribers of Harlequin Intrigue books.

**Are you a current subscriber of Harlequin Intrigue books
and want to receive the larger-print edition?
Call 1-800-873-8635 today!**

* Terms and prices subject to change without notice. Prices do not include applicable taxes. Sales tax applicable in N.Y. Canadian residents will be charged applicable provincial taxes and GST. Offer not valid in Quebec. This offer is limited to one order per household. All orders subject to approval. Credit or debit balances in a customer's account(s) may be offset by any other outstanding balance owed by or to the customer. Please allow 4 to 6 weeks for delivery. Offer available while quantities last.

Your Privacy: Harlequin is committed to protecting your privacy. Our Privacy Policy is available online at www.eHarlequin.com or upon request from the Reader Service. From time to time we make our lists of customers available to reputable third parties who may have a product or service of interest to you. If you would prefer we not share your name and address, please check here. ☐

HI09R

New Year, New Man!

*For the perfect New Year's punch,
blend the following:*

- *One woman determined to find her inner vixen*
- *A notorious—and notoriously hot!—playboy*
- *A provocative New Year's Eve bash*
- *An impulsive kiss that leads to a night of explosive passion!*

When the clock hits midnight Claire Daniels
kisses the guy standing closest to her, but
the kiss doesn't end after the bells stop ringing....

Look for

Moonstruck

by *USA TODAY* bestselling author

JULIE KENNER

Available January

---

red-hot reads

www.eHarlequin.com

HB79518

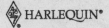
HARLEQUIN®

INTRIGUE®

COMING NEXT MONTH

Available January 12, 2010

#1179 THE SOCIALITE AND THE BODYGUARD
by Dana Marton
Bodyguard of the Month
The ex-commando bodyguard couldn't believe his luck when he was assigned to protect a socialite's poodle. But as he learns that opposites really can attract, he also realizes that his socialite may be the real target of the death threats....

#1180 CLASSIFIED COWBOY by Mallory Kane
The Silver Star of Texas: Comanche Creek
The forensic anthropologist had caught the Texas Ranger's eye years ago, and now he's back for a second chance at love—and at cracking an old case.

#1181 THE SHADOW by Aimée Thurlo
Brotherhood of Warriors
After a series of incidents and threats puts her project—and her life—in jeopardy, she has no choice but to depend on the ex-army ranger to protect her.

#1182 A PERFECT STRANGER by Jenna Ryan
On the run, her new life is put in danger when a gorgeous ex-cop tracks her down and unknowingly exposes her. His conscience won't let him abandon her, and their attraction can only grow stronger... if they survive.

#1183 CASE FILE: CANYON CREEK, WYOMING
by Paula Graves
Cooper Justice
After almost falling victim to a killer, she's the only one who can help a determined Wyoming officer bring him to justice.

#1184 THE SHERIFF OF SILVERHILL by Carol Ericson
The FBI agent returns home to investigate a serial killer, only to find that the sheriff she's working with is the man she had to leave behind.

HICNMBPA1209